'Tell me, Madeline...'

She could see the bitterness burning in his eyes.

'Did you do it just to punish me—or was it that you simply did not care?'

'Your desire to know comes four years too late,' she threw back.

'You're right,' he agreed. 'Four years is a long time to await an answer which really does not interest me. But what does interest me, Madeline,' he persisted harshly, 'is whether those damned four years have managed to make a woman out of the wilful child I thought I loved!'

D1152442

Dear Reader

As Easter approaches, Mills & Boon are delighted to present you with an exciting selection of sixteen new titles. Why not take a trip to our Euromance locations—Switzerland or western Crete, where romance is celebrated in great style! Or maybe you'd care to dip into the story of a family feud or a rekindled love affair? Whatever tickles your fancy, you can always count on love being in the air with Mills & Boon!

The Editor

Michelle Reid grew up on the southern edges of Manchester, the youngest in a family of five lively children. But now she lives in the beautiful county of Cheshire with her busy executive husband and two grown-up daughters. She loves reading, the ballet, and playing tennis when she gets the chance. She hates cooking, cleaning, and despises ironing! Sleep she can do without and produces some of her best written work during the early hours of the morning.

Recent titles by the same author:

HOUSE OF GLASS
LOST IN LOVE

PASSIONATE SCANDAL

BY

MICHELLE REID

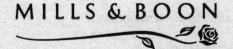

MILLS & BOON LIMITED
ETON HOUSE, 18-24 PARADISE ROAD
RICHMOND, SURREY TW9 1SR

First published in Great Britain 1994
by Mills & Boon Limited

Australian copyright 1994
Philippine copyright 1994
This edition 1994

ISBN 0 263 78447 9

Set in Times Roman 10 on 11½ pt.
01-9404-55726 C

Made and printed in Great Britain

CHAPTER ONE

SEATBELT securely fastened. Seat in its upright position. That distinctive humming sensation in the head that always happened when the cabin slowly depressurised along with their steady descent. And that other very familiar growling sound which said the huge Boeing was throttling back on its final approach into London's Heathrow Airport at last. And suddenly panic erupted from nowhere, drying Madeline's mouth, closing her eyes, catching at her breath and jerking her hands into white-knuckled fists on her trembling lap.

Was she really ready for this?

What a question! she chided herself angrily. What a useless, stupid question to ask herself now, of all times!

Of course she was ready. And even if she wasn't, she would still have come!

Nothing—nothing would stop her from attending Nina's wedding. Not even the reawakening of a sick panic she had thought she'd spent the last four years combating!

Four years, she thought painfully. Surely four years had been quite long enough to spend in exile for her sins, without her having to feel like this? Four years ago she had been just too young and ill-equipped to deal with the pain and humiliation of it all. She had been her own worst enemy then. But she was four years older now, she reminded herself sternly, four years the wiser, and she had gained four full years' much needed maturity and sophistication to help armour herself against

5

whatever waited for her down there beneath those familiar grey clouds of London.

'All right, darling?'

Part of her armour, Madeline admitted as she forced a reassuring smile for her travelling companion. Perry had invited himself along on this trip, and she had hesitated only slightly before accepting his company—whether through conceit or cowardice she wasn't sure. Conceit certainly played a part in her need to show them all at home just how well she could do for herself. And cowardice because she was uncomfortably aware that she was using Perry as an elegant prop for her new image.

An image that was the complete antithesis of her old one.

Perry, she supposed, could be called her latest beau! He was one of the Boston Linburghs. The eldest son and heir in fact to that highly influential and wealthy family. And looked it too, she noted fondly as she studied his smooth lean profile. Hair the colour of wood ash, worn fashionably short, styled to the good shape of his head. His eyes were a warm shade of hazelnut, and his smile the unaffected kind which made him so easy to like.

She and Perry had been a 'thing' for several months now. Their relationship—warmly platonic, she decided, described it best—was useful to both of them, because behind their friendly intimacy they were each nursing the wounds of a broken engagement.

So, when Nina's letter had arrived begging Madeline to come to her wedding, Perry had immediately suggested he come with her.

'I can combine the trip with some business my father needs attending to at our London office. That way, at least I'll be able to to be with you at weekends.' And give you any support you may find you'll need, was his silent addition. She and Perry understood each other very well.

'What's this stepsister of yours like?' he enquired now, turning teasing eyes on her. 'Not one of the wicked kind, is she?'

'Nina?' Madeline gasped. 'Good grief, no!'

If anything, she thought ruefully, she was the wicked stepsister; Nina was the angel.

Madeline was the only child from Edward Gilburn's first marriage, a marriage that had lasted only six stormy years before ending up in a surprisingly amicable divorce considering her parents' track record for doing nothing amicable for each other. The then five-year-old Madeline had remained in England with her father when her mother decided to return to the States to live. Dee, her Boston-born-and-bred mother, had possessed just enough sensitivity to see that parting Madeline from her father would have been nothing short of first-degree murder, since they both doted so much on each other. Dee had not been offended, just philosophical about the situation. Madeline and her father had needed each other more than they needed Dee. So she had packed her lorry loads of baggage and shipped herself back to Boston, where Madeline had commuted on a regular visiting basis ever since.

She had been just eight years old when her father announced his intention to remarry, and she could still remember how determined she had been to hate this unexpected competitor for her father's affections. Then in walked Louise, a vision of fair and gentle loveliness. And by her side, with her small hand clinging to her mother's, stood Nina, tiny will-o'-the-wisp Nina, with her mother's anxious cornflower blue eyes and soft vulnerable mouth. And the very spoiled and wilful Madeline Gilburn had been captivated right there and then.

On looking that far back as the plane's wheels touched smoothly down to earth, Madeline wondered why everyone had been so surprised by her immediate capitulation when over the years she and her father had proved time and time again how much in harmony were their thoughts and feelings. Where one loved, the other invariably loved also.

Which had made it doubly painful for both of them when she and Dominic broke up...

Dominic. Thoughts of Dominic Stanton brought her full circle and back to the very roots of her moment's panic. It was because of him that she had run away to Boston four years ago. And, she acknowledged secretly, it was also because of him that she had decided to come back.

She needed to lay the ghosts of a love long dead.

Customs clearance took ages, but eventually she emerged into the mad crush of the arrivals lounge with her loaded luggage trolley, her blue eyes scanning the sea of faces she encountered, looking for the one she was expecting to see and completely oblivious to the interested glances she was receiving for herself alone.

She was tall and beautifully slender in her tailored suit of pure silk knit, its electric blue colour an exact match to her wide-spaced eyes. Her skin was a little pale after the long hours cooped up in an aeroplane, but nothing could dim its natural purity. Her long blue-black hair had been confined in a braided coronet for the journey, and had arrived at the end of it looking as sleek and sophisticated as it had when she'd set off more than twelve hours ago. She was the kind of woman who stood out in a crowd. Destined to belong to someone special. Exclusive.

The man walking at her side suited her. His air of high breeding and easy sophistication showed clearly. His smooth fairness complemented her dark sleekness. Two very sophisticated people.

'Madeline!'

Her head twisted, blue eyes alighting on the tall distinguished figure of her father, and on a soft cry she moved eagerly into his arms.

'You're late,' he complained after releasing her from a suffocating bear-hug of an embrace. 'Over an hour late coming in, and another hour getting through those infernal Customs!'

Madeline smiled and kissed his cheek. 'Don't knock the tight security,' she scolded him. 'It's all done for our own safety.'

'Hmph,' was his only answer to that as he held her out at arm's length so he could look at her. 'You're looking good enough to eat,' he decided, 'though how you manage to after that lousy journey confounds me.'

'Mummy comes in useful for some things, you know,' she grinned. Expecting and getting another disparaging 'Hmph'.

There was very little love lost between her parents. Her father saw Dee as a very beautiful but empty-headed social doll, and Dee saw her father as a brusque, insensitive tyrant. The only place they met in any harmony was where their daughter was concerned, and even there they begged to differ—over all points but her happiness.

'Now, where's this young man your mother's been telling me so much about?'

Turning in her father's arms, Madeline searched Perry out, to find he had been joined by a big dark-haired man who was greeting him like an old friend.

'Forman!' she cried in surprise.

The newcomer grinned and came over to kiss her cheek. She had met Forman Goulding several times in Boston. He was a big dark man with the kind of hard masculine looks she tended to shy away from these days. He was also Perry's cousin and the member of the family who took care of their European interests.

It was with Forman that Perry was going to stay during his stay in London, coming to Madeline in Lambourn during the weekends only. By the time all the introductions had been made, her father had invited Forman down to Lambourn with Perry whenever he wished to join them, then they were all moving outside to her father's Bentley, with Rogers his chauffeur standing by the boot waiting to receive her luggage, and in front of it a long low growling monster of a car which could only belong to Forman Goulding.

Perry took Madeline in his arms and kissed her gently, promising to be with her in Lambourn by Saturday lunchtime.

'That was a fine show of affection,' her father commented once they were seated in the car and on their way.

'Was it?' Madeline murmured, then subtly turned the conversation by demanding to know how everyone was, her eyes warm on him as she listened to all the latest news.

At fifty-five he was still a strikingly attractive man with his head of thick wavy hair which had gone prematurely white in his twenties. He was a man who carried the power he wielded around with him like a banner. Dominic had once described him as a man who totally lacked caution but possessed the luck of the devil to compensate. Reluctant though Madeline was to agree with anything Dominic Stanton said, she had to agree with that particular observation. Her father took risks in business guaranteed to rock the City back on its heels in horror. The fact that he invariably made the right move placed him high on the respect rating with people in the speculative business. Few scoffed at a Gilburn idea. Nobody dared underestimate him. He was just too sharp, too shrewd.

'And what's this Charles Waverley like?' she asked when her father concluded the local news without mentioning Nina's new fiancé. 'I can't imagine our own little Nina getting married and leaving the fold,' she added drily. 'She was always such a timid little home bird.'

'Charles is perfect for Nina,' her father assured her. 'He possesses a natural desire to love and cherish, which is all we can ever ask of the man who wins our Nina. Their marriage will be a good one,' he asserted confidently.

A weight pressing down on her heart kept Madeline silent while she diminished it. It was nothing new to her to feel this terrible burden constricting her chest whenever she thought of love and marriage. It was something she'd had to learn to live with—and control so no one else knew it was there. Love held only bitter memories for her, painful experiences she wouldn't wish on her worst enemy. Marriage meant commitment. An honest declaration of love undying. She had once known love, thought the offer of marriage gave her that commitment. But she had been wrong. And she never wanted Nina to know that same pain, that same anguished desolation.

'And Louise—how is she?' she asked next.

'Very well,' her father said positively. 'Beautiful and well,' he added with all the satisfaction of a man who adored his lovely wife to distraction. Louise suited the blustery Edward Gilburn far better than Madeline's own mother had. With Louise he had a chance to utilise that softer side of his nature which otherwise would never be seen. No one would think of being cruel or tyrannical towards Louise. She was just too soft and vulnerable. 'And eager to have you back home,' he finished warmly.

Madeline didn't doubt it. Louise had been a wonderful surrogate mother to her throughout her formative years. And she had done it without coming between daughter and father or outlawing Dee.

'She had your rooms completely refurbished as a surprise for you—then sat down and worried herself silly that she should have left them as you remembered them, and had us all frantic in case she decided to change them back again in the hopes that you wouldn't notice! Nina managed to stop her.' He sounded heartily relieved. 'She told her that the new Madeline I've been telling them all about would hate to sleep in a candy-pink room with frills and flounces!'

Would she? Madeline laughed dutifully, but felt a heavy sense of loss inside, as if the old Madeline had died, and this new one was just a stand-in. Would other people see her as a stranger now, someone they had to learn to know all over again? She shuddered at the thought. She had just grown up, that was all. Albeit late.

Watching her covertly, Edward Gilburn read more in his daughter's studiously placid features than she would like. He had worried terribly about her when she first went to Boston four years ago. Dee had been marvellous with her, he had to admit. She'd refused to let their daughter mope, dragging her—literally sometimes— protesting miserably out to face the human race and learn to deal with it again. But he had feared what kind of person was going to emerge from the ashes of this brutal kind of therapy. He had been relieved to find Madeline slowly learning to cope during his regular visits to see her in Boston. But he could not say he was exactly happy with the final result of the four-year influence of her rather superficial mother.

Where had all that sparkling eagerness to meet life full on gone? he wondered in grim exasperation. That wild and wonderful love of life which made her the captivating creature she was at eighteen? Trust Dee to bleed it all out of her, he thought grimly.

And, not for the first time, he cursed Dominic Stanton for making it necessary for his baby to place herself in the hands of her mother.

'Nina was worried you might not come,' he put in quietly.

'Because of Dominic, you mean?' As usual, Madeline went directly for the point, and Edward smiled to himself. Dee obviously hadn't managed to curb that natural habit. Then the smile went awry when he remembered how that painfully open honesty of hers had made her broken love affair with Dominic all the harder for her to bear. She had not been able to seek solace in lying to herself, and the truth had been so dreadfully hard to endure. 'I didn't know I'd given such a feeble impression of myself.'

'You didn't, darling, and you know it.' Her father's hand came out to take hers, squeezing it gently.

'What Dominic did to me was cruel.' Madeline said flatly. 'But what I did to him was unforgivable. Neither of us came out of it well. It took me a whole year to acknowledge that,' she admitted on a small smile. 'And a bit of brutal talking from Mummy,' she added drily. 'She was brutal all around, when I come to think of it.' She shrugged, slender shoulders moving up and down beneath the immaculate silk jacket. 'Was that your doing?' She looked enquiringly at her father. 'Did you advise her not to let me wallow?'

His face gave him away, and Madeline smiled again. If anyone knew how best to deal with her, then it was this man. 'Thank you,' she leaned over to kiss his cheek. 'Your instincts rarely let you down, do they?'

'They did where Dominic was concerned,' he muttered gruffly. He had liked and respected Dominic Stanton. So much so that he'd encouraged his love affair with Madeline from its conception. Everyone concerned had, the Stantons just as eagerly as the Gilburns. It had been a beautiful dream while it lasted. 'I'll never forgive myself for my part in encouraging you.' He voiced his grim thoughts out loud.

'You really had no say in what I did, you know,' Madeline drily pointed out. And he grinned because he knew as well as she did that when Madeline wanted something badly enough she went all out to get it. And she had wanted Dominic, so badly that it still hurt just to remember. 'We were simply wrong for each other,' she stated flatly. 'And we should perhaps be thankful that we found out soon enough. Does Charles Waverley run a successful racing stable?' Once again, she deftly changed the subject.

'Very. He trained last year's Derby winner...'

There were going to be some surprised faces around Lambourn in the near future, Edward Gilburn ruefully judged as he watched the sleek mask of sophistication drop smoothly into place on his daughter's face. And found himself yearning for a time when a black-haired, wicked-eyed gypsy had danced all over his peace of mind. A time when Nina had captivated, and Madeline shocked. While Nina had sat sewing her fine seam, filling his heart with a gentle gladness for being allowed to take the place of her dead father, Madeline would be off on some wild prank or other which would inevitably bring his wrath tumbling down on her unrepentant head—followed by his secret respect. She rode like the devil, played every sport there was going with panache. And later, when she grew into a wild and wilful young woman, she'd run rings around all the poor besotted young men who fell for a pair of wicked blue eyes and a mane of wild black hair.

Dee had despaired of ever taming her then, he recalled. She would send letters home with Madeline after one of her Boston visits, enquiring in her oh, so sarcastic way if Edward was raising their daughter as a delinquent for any specific reason. But even Dee had had to admit that Madeline drew the opposite sex to her like bees to honey, that she was exciting to be with. Madeline possessed a fierce will of her own, but she was also able to laugh at herself, and not many could do that.

Dominic hadn't laughed, the damned fool! If he had— if only he had laughed that fateful night of the country club ball, then maybe Madeline wouldn't have run away, and maybe she would not be sitting next to him now, talking with the bland aplomb of the well trained socialite.

He preferred the other girl, the one who would have been bouncing up and down beside him right now, brimming with excitement, plans, driving him demented with the pranks she intended pulling on her friends.

Or maybe she wouldn't, he then revised thoughtfully. Maybe time alone would have taken the spirited child out of Madeline. Perhaps Dominic Stanton had only accelerated a natural progression—though he didn't think so. He knew his daughter well, knew what kind of devil drove her, because the self-same one had driven him. It had taken him over forty years to learn to tame his own. He hadn't expected Madeline to do it any quicker.

No, Dominic had done that, taught her how to think before she acted; hide instead of being her true exciting self!

* * *

They stood like a formal reception party, Madeline noted
drily as the car slowed and stopped in front of the grey-
stoned country manor house where Louise, Nina and a
serious-faced man stood waiting for them at the bottom
of the wide stone steps.

Louise looked no different than she had the last time
Madeline had seen her four years ago now. Small, and
neat-figured, she still had hair that shone that wonderful spun-gold colour, and her smile was still that in-
finitely gentle one Madeline had first encountered at the
age of eight. Nina had altered, though, she noted with
a small shock. Her stepsister had grown more beautiful
in the four intervening years, her pale gold hair a short
cap of enchanting curls around her angelic face. And
that had to be Charles Waverley, she decided as she
turned her attention to the only stranger in their midst.
Tall, weatherbeaten, with the whipcord-lean frame of a
working farmer, he stood head and shoulders above both
women. There was an expression of solemn reserve about
his chocolate-brown eyes.

And it was at him that she smiled first. Why, she wasn't
quite sure, except that she knew somehow that it was
what Nina would want her to do, make this man she had
fallen in love with know she welcomed him into their
small family fold.

She saw the uncertain glance he sent Nina before he
levelled his gaze back on her, and also saw the hint of
relief, as if he'd just taken some terribly important test
and was now glad it was over.

'Maddie, darling!' It was Louise who came forward
to envelop her in her warm embrace. 'Oh, it's so wonderful to have you home!' She pushed her to arm's length
in much the same way her father had done earlier at the
airport, her smile rather watery. 'And looking so different, too!' she exclaimed. 'So frightfully sophisticated!'

'Nice to be back, Louise,' she answered earnestly, somehow unable to return the effusive greeting. It'll come back, she told herself firmly, frowning inwardly at her own reticence. It was only now as she stood here with these people she had spent so many years of her life with that she noticed the restraint she had learnt to apply on herself. 'And you haven't changed in the slightest,' she made an effort to sound natural. 'I hope Nina won't mind if I tell you I had to take a second look to tell which of you was which!'

'You've earned yourself a kiss for that,' Nina said promptly, coming to replace her mother in Madeline's arms. 'I can't think of a better compliment than to know I look like Mummy. Hello, Maddie,' she added huskily, looking up at her with gentle, loving eyes. 'Have you missed us?'

'Every single day,' she assured, unwilling to tell the truth and admit that she had found it necessary to her own survival to dismiss all that was even vaguely English from her mind for those first few years. 'And you look wonderful. Would that have anything to do with this rather dishy man I see standing guard behind you?' she teased.

Nina blushed, and turned to draw Charles Waverley closer. 'This is Charles, Madeline,' she gravely introduced. 'And you have to like each other on sight, or I shall be miserable.'

Madeline found herself looking once again into those serious brown eyes, and held out her hand. 'Well,' she said frankly, 'I shall promise to like you on sight, Charles, so long as you can promise me you'll take precious care of Nina.'

'A promise I won't find it difficult to keep.' He smiled, and took her outstretched hand.

'Let's get inside, shall we?' Edward Gilburn's gruff voice broke in. 'Come on, Charles,' he took his future son-in-law's arm. 'Women are notoriously silly when it comes to hellos and goodbyes. Let's you and I go and find a nice glass of something while they talk each other's tails off.'

With a laugh, the three women followed them indoors, and proceeded to do exactly what Edward Gilburn had predicted by chatting madly—or, more correctly, Nina and Louise did the chattering. Madeline simply smiled a lot and put the odd word in now and then when required. They didn't seem to notice her reserve, though she did.

It will come, she repeated to herself on a small frown. It was only natural that she should feel strange with them after a four-year separation. The old natural camaraderie would return soon enough once she'd settled back in...

CHAPTER TWO

BUT it didn't. And it was a relief to escape.

Madeline turned Minty, her chestnut mare, towards the river and cantered off. The clouds which had welcomed her home to England had all but cleared away now, leaving a bright full April moon shining in the night sky above her. It wasn't late, barely nine o'clock, but it was cold, cold enough to warrant the big sheepskin jacket she had pulled on over her jeans and sweater.

Her decision to take a ride alone had been met with consternation, but they'd let her go. It wasn't as if they were concerned for her safety. Madeline had been riding over this part of the countryside since she was old enough to climb on to the back of a horse. It was just that they were hurt by her need to get away from them so soon after her arrival home.

But she could not have taken any more tonight.

Within an hour of arriving she'd begun to feel like an invalid home on convalescence because of the way they all seemed to tiptoe around her, around subjects they'd obviously decided between them were strictly taboo, watching her with guarded if loving eyes. By the time another hour had gone by, she had been straining at the leash to escape. Dinner had been an ordeal, her tension and their uncertainty of her acting against each other to make conversation strained and stilted.

She'd blamed her restlessness on jet-lag when she saw their expressions. And they'd smiled, bright, false, tension-packed smiles. 'Of course!' her father had exclaimed—too heartily. 'A ride is just what you need to make you feel at home again!' Louise had agreed, while Nina just looked at her with huge eyes.

Madeline's soft mouth tightened. So, she'd hurt them all, but she couldn't do a single thing about it just yet. Four years was a long time. They all had adjustments to make—her family more than herself, because she was what she was, and nothing like the girl who had left here four years ago.

They were all exactly the same, though, she told herself heavily. They hadn't changed at all.

Minty's hoofs pounded on the frozen ground, and Madeline crouched down low on her back, giving herself up to the sheer exhilaration of the ride as they galloped across the dark countryside. The further she got away from the house, the more relaxed she began to feel, as if the distance weakened the family strings that had been busily trying to wrap themselves around her aching heart.

She didn't know why she felt this way, only that she did. From the moment she'd stepped out of the car, she'd felt stifled, haunted almost, by memories none of them could even begin to contemplate.

A sharp bend in the river was marked by a thick clump of trees standing big and dark against a navy blue sky. She skirted the wood until she found the old path which led down to the river itself, allowing Minty to pick her own way to what was one of their old haunts: a small clearing among the trees, where the springy turf grew to the edge of the steep riverbank.

She loved this place, she thought with a sigh, sliding down from Minty's back to stand, simply absorbing the peace and tranquillity of her surroundings. Especially at night, when the river ran dark and silent, and the trees stood like sentinels, big and brooding. Her father had used to call her a creature of the night. 'An owl,' he used to say, 'while Nina is a lark.'

The full moon was blanching the colour out of everything, surrounding her in tones of black and grey, except for the river, where it formed slinky silver patterns on the silent mass as it moved with a ghostly kind of grace.

Letting the bridle fall so that Minty could put down her head to graze, Madeline shoved her hands into the pockets of her old sheepskin coat and sucked in a deep breath of sharp, crisp, clean air then let it out again slowly, feeling little by little the tension leave her body. It wasn't fair—she knew she was being unfair. They were good, kind, loving people who only wanted the best for her and for her to be happy.

But how could she tell them that she'd forgotten what happiness was? Real happiness at any rate, the kind she had once embraced without really bothering to think about it.

Sighing, she moved towards the edge of the bank where she could hear the water softly lapping the pebbly ground several feet below her.

On the other side of the river, hidden behind another thick clump of trees, the old Courtney place stood dark and intimidating. She could just make out its crooked chimneystacks as the moon slid lazily over them. It was an old Elizabethan thing, let to go over the years until it had gained the reputation of being haunted. Its owner, Major Courtney, had done nothing to refute the claims. He was a recluse, an eccentric straight out of the Victorian era who had guarded his privacy so fiercely that in her mad youth Madeline had loved to torment him by creeping into his overgrown garden just so he would come running out with his shotgun at the ready.

Shocking creature! she scolded herself now, but with a smile which was pure 'old' Madeline.

The silence was acting like a balm, soothing away a bleakness she had been struggling with from the moment she had stepped into the house this afternoon. She knew exactly why it was there. Her problem was how to come to terms with it.

She had not expected Dominic's presence to be so forcefully stamped into everything she rested her eyes upon.

'Damn him,' she whispered softly to the night, and huddled deeper into her coat.

'Another step, and you'll fall down the bank,' a quiet voice warned from somewhere behind her.

The moon slid behind a lonely cloud. Blackness engulfed her suddenly, and Madeline let out a strangled cry, her heart leaping to her mouth as she jumped, almost doing exactly what that voice warned against and plunging down the riverbank in sheer fright.

Heart hammering, the breath stripped clean from her body, she spun around, eyes wide and frightened as they searched the inky blackness for a glimpse of a body to go with the voice.

Another horse stood calmly beside Minty. And Madeline realised that she had been so engrossed in her own thoughts that she hadn't heard the other rider come up. But she could see no one, and a fine chilling thread of alarm began slinking along her spine while she stood there breathless and still, the sudden deathly silence filling her ears, drying her mouth while her eyes flicked anxiously around the dark clearing.

By legend, this was highwayman country. And she could conjure up at least three gruesome tales of ghostly sightings in these parts. She'd always laughed them off before—while secretly wishing she could witness something supernatural. Now, she was rueing that foolish wish.

The horses shifted, bridles jingling as they nudged against each other. Madeline blinked, her eyes stinging with the effort it took to pierce the pitch-blackness.

'Who's there?' she demanded shakily.

'Who do you think?' drawled a mocking voice.

It was then, as she caught the lazy mockery, the dark velvet resonance of the voice, that the fear went flying as a new and far more disturbing emotion took over, making her hands clench in her pockets as she saw a movement over to the right of the horses.

A tall figure of a man detached itself from the shadow of a tree, looking more wicked than any highwayman could to Madeline's agitated mind. She had known him to come upon her like this many times, using shock tactics to heighten her awareness of him. He was that kind of man. A man who thrived on others' uncertainty.

'So, the prodigal has returned at last.'

'Hello, Dom,' she said, forcing herself to sound cool and unaffected by his sudden presence, even as her nerve-ends scrambled desperately for something she refused to acknowledge. 'What brings you out here tonight of all nights?'

The moon came out from behind its cloud, and his smile flashed white in his shadowed face. 'The same thing as you, I should imagine,' he answered, close enough for her to see the clean taut lines of his handsome face. 'Hello, Maddie,' he belatedly responded.

He seemed to loom like the trees, tall and dark, black jeans and a heavy black sweater exaggerating the muscled power of his body. Everything about Dominic Stanton was in general larger than life, she mused acidly. Including his vows of undying love.

Abruptly she turned away from him, a hard pang of pain twisting in her ribs. They had used to meet here often once. It had been their place—among several others along this eerie riverbank. She would always arrive first, the more eager, she bitterly recalled. And he would come out of the darkness to take her in his——

A hand touched her shoulder. She reacted violently, his unexpected touch coinciding so closely with her thoughts that she took a jerky step back, and felt the riverbank tilt dangerously beneath her feet.

'You stupid fool!' he growled, fingers digging into her shoulders as he yanked her on to safer ground. 'What do you think I'm going to do—rape you?'

Rape? A noise left her throat like a hysterical choke. Since when had he had to resort to rape with her? Surely it had been the other way around.

'Let go of me,' she insisted, disgusted with herself because even now, after four long years, one look at him and everything she had in her was clamouring in hungry greeting, sending her pulses leaping wildly.

His eyes still looked down at her with that same passionate intensity; his mouth was still firm-lipped and sensual. He still stood eight inches above her, still exuded that same hardcore sexuality that had always driven her mad with wanting—and still had the ability to stir her wayward nature.

She hated him for that. Hated him for making it happen.

His hands left her instantly, and she almost sagged in groaning relief. 'Don't worry,' he said tightly. 'I want to touch you probably less than you want to feel my touch on you.'

'W-what are you doing here?' she demanded, wanting to rub her arms where his fingers had dug in—not because he'd hurt her, but because her flesh was stinging as if she'd just been burned.

'To see you, what else?' He moved back a step to thrust his own hands out of sight in the tight pockets of his jeans. 'Four years is a long time not to set eyes on the woman who made a public spectacle of me.'

She had made a public spectacle of him? Madeline almost laughed out loud. 'As I remember it,' she smiled bitterly, 'it was the other way around.'

'Not from where I was standing, it wasn't,' he grunted. 'Humiliated by a spoiled if beautiful black-haired brat who has never given a care for anyone but herself!'

'Thank you,' she drawled. 'It's so nice to know how fondly my then fiancé thought of me.'

'As nice as it was for me to find out what a faithless fiancée you were to me?'

Madeline visibly flinched, guilt and shame four years in the nurturing holding the breath congealed inside her lungs. And she had to look away from him, unable to defend herself against that ruthless thrust. There was just too much truth in it.

Silence fell hard and tight between them, and they stood stiffly in the moonlit clearing, neither seeming to know what to say next to hurt the other. It was amazing how the antipathy was still there throbbing like a war drum between them. It should have dulled a little by now, at least withered into a mutual dislike maybe, but it hadn't. And this meeting could be happening the night after the country club ball for the way they were reacting to one another, and the intervening years might as well as not have gone by.

The moon hung like a silver lantern above their heads, etching out each harshly handsome line of his smooth lean face: the silky black bars of his eyebrows, almost touching as he glowered down at her; his eyes glinting at her from beneath those dark thick lashes; his slender nose, long and arrogant, just like the man. And his mouth, she noted lastly. Just a thin taut line of contempt which even then could not disguise its in-built sensuality.

'Four years,' Dominic muttered suddenly. 'And you still look the same bewitching child. Still more beautiful than any woman ought to be.'

Something inside her twisted in pained yearning, and she went to turn away from him, only to find her arms caught once again in his bruising grip. 'Not yet,' he bit out. 'You're not going to escape again just yet. Tell me, Madeline . . .' He pushed his angry face closer to her own so that she could see the bitterness burning in his eyes, feel it pulsing right through him. 'Did you do it just to punish me? Or was it that you simply did not care?'

'Your desire to know comes four years too late,' she threw back, lifting her chin to let her cool gaze clash with his angry one.

He looked ready to shake her out of her coolness, and certainly his fingers tightened their grip on her arms. Then he suddenly seemed to think better of it. 'You're right,' he agreed. 'Four years is a long time to await an answer which really does not interest me. But what does interest me, Madeline,' he persisted harshly, 'is whether Boston and those damned four years have managed to make a woman out of the wilful child I thought I loved!'

She should have expected it, Madeline realised a moment later. She should have read it in the sudden flash of those coldly burning eyes, seen it in the tension of his hard mouth just before it landed punishingly on top of her own. But she hadn't, too shaken by her own disturbing reactions accurately to interpret his, and his warm breath rasped against her cold mouth as he went from the verbal attack to the physical in one swift angry movement.

Stunned into total stillness, she just stood in front of him, his fingers biting into her arms through the padded warmth of her sheepskin coat as he held her tight against him. And the angry pressure of his mouth crushed her lips back against her teeth, forcing them apart and drawing memories from her that she would far rather have left banished to the dark recesses of her mind.

And as each lonely sense began to stir inside her, awakening to the only source ever to bring them to life, she began to fight, fight like hell for release—aware of his angry passion, of her own reaching up to match it, and wanting neither.

Never again! she told herself desperately as she strained frantically away from him. Never again!

'Home half a day,' he muttered, lifting his head to glare at her through eyes shot silver with a strange mixture of rage and anguish. 'And already I can't——'

The words died, choked off by a thickened throat as his mouth came back to hers. He lifted a hand to bury his fingers in the silken softness of her hair, drawing her head back, forcing her face up to his own. His other arm was like steel around her waist, clamping her to him, and the helpless groan he gave against her mouth wrenched an answering one from herself.

The kiss went on and on, nothing kind or loving in the cruel assault, but slowly she felt her control slipping away from her, felt her senses begin to hum with a need to respond. And suddenly they were kissing frenziedly, straining against each other, lost in the turmoil which had always been an exciting part of their relationship four years ago. When Dominic had allowed it to happen, that was, which wasn't often.

Reality came crashing back with the memory, and she dragged her mouth away from his, her own bitterness aimed entirely at herself because once again she had fallen for his easy passion—a passion she knew from experience he could switch on and off like a tap.

'It's funny how we should both end up on this particular spot by the river tonight of all nights,' he murmured against the heated smoothness of her cheek. 'I seem to still possess that special antenna where you're concerned, Madeline. I think I knew the moment you stepped back on to British soil. What does that admission do to your quaking heart, I wonder?' he taunted silkily. 'Does it make it beat all the faster?'

The flat of his hand suddenly came out to press firmly against the heaving mound of her breast where her heart was racing madly beneath the thick padding of her sheepskin coat. And she gasped.

'Stop it,' she hissed, trying to push him away. 'Stop it, Dominic—please!'

'Why?' he taunted. 'You love it! You always did!'

His mouth crushed down on to hers again with one last angry kiss, then suddenly she was free, standing dazed and swaying in front of him as he pushed himself away from her as violently as he had taken hold.

'The next plane to Boston leaves in the morning,' she heard him say quite coldly. 'If you aren't on it, Madeline, I shall take it that you're prepared to stay and fight this time, instead of running away like the coward I never thought you to be.'

Then he was gone, striding away and leaping on to his horse before she had a chance to absorb the full meaning of his words.

The dull throb of galloping hoofs kept time with the thud of her pounding heart as she remained standing there, staring blankly at the spot he had last been standing in, her confused mind half wondering if she had imagined the whole incredible scene!

God knew, she'd dreamed of confrontations similar to this one often enough in the last four years—struggled with the same emotions clamouring inside her now. But never had she thought of Dominic being the one throwing out ultimatums. It had always been the other way around, she the injured one and he the one to grovel and plead.

Was she going to run away again?

The idea certainly appealed to her as she forced her quivering body to move. Meeting him unexpectedly like this had shaken her to the very core. And the knowledge that she was no more invulnerable to him now than she had been four years ago frightened her into seriously considering going back to Boston before he could really manage to hurt her.

Revenge, she realised grimly as she climbed on to Minty's back. Dominic had just warned her that he was out for revenge, for what he called her humiliation of him.

Surely he had to see that he'd already had his revenge on her? In her mind they were quits. And this angry meeting should never have taken place.

'Damn you, Dominic Stanton,' she whispered into the icy darkness, her heart aching in so many different ways. 'Damn you to hell.'

Damn him, she was still cursing him over an hour later as she restlessly paced her bedroom floor, her hands dug into the pockets of her blue satin robe.

Louise had showed her usual good taste in the refurbishment of her rooms, she acknowledged on a defiant snub to her troubled thoughts. Gone were the hearts and flowers, and soft toning blues and greys had replaced childish pinks, with the occasional splash of deep violet in acknowledgement of her own love of passionate colours. The walls were plain-painted instead of pattern-papered, the furnishings either replaced or re-covered to reflect the more mature woman, yet the touch of femininity was here, in the dozens of lace-edged satin cushions scattered about the place. Her old single bed had been replaced by a grand-looking double one with a beautiful silver-grey satin quilt thrown over it, appliquéd in blue and lilac silks. The carpet was grey and thick beneath her bare feet, the drapes the palest blue with tie-backs to match the bedcover.

Madeline sat down on her dressing stool, absently picking up her brush to stroke it through the tangled mass of recently wind-blown hair. She looked tired; dark smudges were spoiling the soft skin around her eyes. Her body felt heavy with fatigue, yet her limbs refused to stay still, twitching and forcing her to keep moving when she really wanted to flop into a blissfully deep sleep.

She was experienced enough in the side-effects of long-distance travel to know it was going to take her several days to adjust. But it wasn't jet-lag bothering her tonight, she admitted heavily to herself. It was Dominic.

He hadn't changed, not one small inch of him, inside or out. He was still big and lean and powerfully attractive. He still possessed that strong sexual allure about him that had always drawn her to him.

Could still kiss like the devil.

Her body responded, curling up into a tight tingling coil then springing open to spray those tingles all over her, and she sucked in a sharp breath, half impatience, half desperation.

It would have been better if Dominic had never seen her as anything but his sister's best friend; then he would not have become the bitter man she had met down by the river tonight, and she would not be suffering the same old calamity of emotions he had always managed to stir inside her from that first moment he had looked at her and seen Madeline the woman and not the aggravating child.

She had scampered in and out of his life for years before that, seeing him as nothing more than Vicky's big brother whose ten-year age difference placed him on a different plane from that which she had existed on. He had been one of them—the grown-up set she so loved to torment. And Vicky had loved to watch her do it because she herself was so in awe of her big brother that she didn't dare antagonise him as Maddie had no qualms about doing.

Then the change had come. Circumstances had meant that she and Dominic hadn't seen each other for almost two years, Dom because he was busy at his father's bank, travelling the world as high-stepping financiers did, and she because she was busy studying for exams or commuting more often to Boston. And they had just seemed to miss—like ships in the night, she thought now with bitter wryness.

It was during the month of her eighteenth birthday that they met for the first time as adults. It was one of those long, lazy June days when the sun blazed down from an unblemished sky and the air lay so hot and still that she and Vicky had decided to laze around the Stanton swimming-pool for the afternoon.

Madeline's skin already glowed with the rich golden tan from a recent Florida holiday with her family—her American family, that was—her mother, Lincoln, her second husband, and his two teenage children from his first marriage. She enjoyed being with them all for the month she spent there, but, as always, was glad to come home to Lambourn, and had been back only a few days when she donned her black and white striped one-piece swimsuit which showed more flesh than it hid and made Vicky green with envy for her luscious tan.

'That figure of yours should be censored,' her friend complained, eyeing the way the fashionable suit moulded Madeline's slender frame from the firm fullness of her breasts to the high cutaway sides which made an open statement about the long sleek length of her legs.

'Pocket Venuses bring out the male instinct to protect,' she answered soothingly, studying Vicky's demure little frame with her own brand of envy. Next to Vicky—and Nina, come to that—Madeline had always felt a bit like an Amazon. She had what Louise called an exotic figure. It didn't inure her much to the softly rounded curves she had, but, never the type to chew on her lip in yearning for what she saw as too much of everything, she accepted her lot and got on with life in her usual happy-go-lucky way.

She had just got up from her padded lounger and executed a neat dive into the pool, and was swimming lazily up and down when another splash alerted her to the fact that she was no longer alone in the pool. She expected to see Vicky's streaky brown head emerge beside her, and was therefore surprised when the dark, attractive features of Dominic grinned white-toothed at her instead, water streaming down his tanned body, muscles rippling everywhere, cording his strong neck where it met broad shoulders.

'Now, what have we here?' he murmured silkily, his warm grey eyes glinting with mischief. 'A real live water nymph in our pool? Does she cast wicked spells, I wonder?'

For all Madeline had been the one to torment Dominic over the years, he wasn't averse to giving her a taste of her own medicine when in the mood—and he was clearly in the mood that day.

'Wicked ones,' she grinned, surprised to feel so pleased to see him. 'So watch it,' she warned, wagging a lazy finger his way. 'Or I may decide to turn you into a frog. And then what would all the lovely Lambourn ladies do without the rakish Dominic Stanton to send their poor hearts all a-flutter?'

He grinned and so did she—then with her usual impulsiveness she turned a somersault and dived beneath the water, grabbing at his foot as she went so that she could trail him down with her, watching the disconcertment on his face as he tried to tug his captured foot free, air bubbles escaping all around them.

He was a big man, but Madeline was strong and determined. In the end, he had to grab her wrist and make her release him, and they both came to the surface gasping for air.

'God, you haven't changed much, have you?' he choked, flinging back his head to clear his soaked hair from his face.

Madeline saw the measuring glint in his eyes, squealed when she correctly interpreted its vengeful meaning, and made a flailing dive for the side of the pool. She didn't make it. Dominic caught her by the waist and lifted her up high above him, laughing at her helplessness as water streamed down her sun-browned skin.

Then he wasn't laughing but looking, those piercing grey eyes of his warm on her body, taking in its new maturity, the unconscious sensuality in the way she arched away from him in an attempt to free herself, her breasts thrusting up and outwards, the hard press of her extended nipples clearly etched against the fine Lycra material of her suit, her head thrown back so her hair turned into a thick curtain of wet black silk which trailed in the water behind her.

He muttered something beneath his breath, and Madeline stopped struggling to glance questioningly at him.

It was then that she saw it—the change from teasing big brother to sexually stimulated male. His eyes were narrowed and his body tense. And slowly—slowly he lowered her down the length of him, letting her feel—and feeling for himself—the electric response as their wet bodies brushed enticingly against each other.

Their faces came level, and Madeline stared in blushing confusion at him. His mouth twisted, a self-mockery masking out the sensual awareness. Yet he did not immediately release her, Instead his hands went on an outrageous exploration of her body beneath the surface of the water. Breathlessly, she let him, her eyes fixed on his face as awareness began to pulse between them.

'When did you get back?' Vicky's sleep-slurred voice broke into their absorption in each other, breaking them apart with an abruptness that was a message in itself. They glanced up to find her yawning lazily, completely unaware of the sudden tension fizzing in her pool. She blinked at her brother, then repeated the question, adding, 'Daddy said you wouldn't be back until tomorrow.'

He turned away from Madeline, and instantly she dived below the surface of the water, swimming quickly away until she had put the full width of the pool between them, her senses in turmoil, a confusion over what had just happened making her feel peculiarly dizzy.

'I finished quicker than I thought I would, so I caught an earlier flight home.' He answered his sister levelly enough. 'How are you, pug-face?' he enquired teasingly as he levered himself out of the pool.

Suddenly and disturbingly aware of her own body, Madeline found that it took all her courage to make her climb out of the pool. And the fact that she was actually blushing made Dominic's eyes glint mockingly at her as he watched her fumble with her towelling wrap while seemingly totally engrossed in a conversation with his sister.

'Have dinner with me tonight,' he murmured later under cover of Vicky's light chatter.

Feeling shy for perhaps the very first time in her life, she shook her head, not at all sure she wanted to continue what had begun in the pool. 'I don't——'

'Please.' His hand curled about her wrist, stopping her mid-refusal. His touch acted like a bee-sting to her system and she gasped as the blood began to burn in her veins. Even Vicky had gone silent, watching with growing comprehension what was happening between her best friend and her big brother.

'Dinner, that's all,' he repeated, then added in a soft-voiced challenge, 'Where's that spirit of adventure you're so famous for?'

Well, it was dead now, thought the four-years-older Madeline. Killed by the hand that had once loved to feed it. Ruthlessly crushed by a man who took his revenge on a stupid impulsive child in a way which had instantly cured her of a lot of things. But most of all it had cured her of her silly belief that love conquered all. And she no longer believed in love at all now—not the all-consuming passionate kind, anyway.

CHAPTER THREE

MADELINE rang Vicky the next day.

'You're back!' came the excited proclamation.

'I think so,' she murmured drily, 'although I'm not certain all of me is here, if you know what I mean.'

'Jet-lag,' Vicky recognised. 'Are you too tired to meet me today?'

'Do you mean you may manage to fit me in?' Madeline teased. 'I believe you have certain—commitments which curtail your freedom these days.'

'You've heard,' Vicky grunted. 'Who told you— Nina?'

'My father, actually,' Madeline corrected, unaware of the sudden tension on the other end of the line. 'He's rather proud of you, Vicky,' she went on oblivious. 'Said you're making quite a name for yourself at the bank.'

'Against all the odds,' Vicky added drily, knowing Madeline was aware of how determined she had been to join the family bank—and how equally determined her father had been to keep her out of it. 'It took me three years' hard graft at the uni and a lot of rows before he caved in. But even he couldn't turn a blind eye to the distinctions I got with my degree. I have been an official Stanton bank employee for just over a year now,' she proudly announced. 'Dom says I...' Her voice trailed off, silent horror singing down the line between them.

Madeline sighed inwardly, seeing the irony in the way everyone seemed determined to skirt around all mention of Dominic Stanton while the man himself felt no qualms in making his presence more than felt! 'Dom says—what?' she prompted gently.

'He—he says it's my sexy behind that draws in the new accounts,' Vicky mumbled uncomfortably.

'Why, do you wriggle it at every potential client?' Madeline asked, damning the odd tightness she felt in her chest when she visualised Dominic's flashing grin as he issued that small tease to his sister.

'Only at the male ones,' Vicky chuckled, the tension easing out of her voice again. 'What about Saturday night on the town if you don't fancy making the trip into London today?'

'No can do, I'm afraid.' Madeline apologised. 'I have a friend coming to stay.'

'Perry Linburgh?' Vicky quizzed.

'How did you find that out so quickly?' Madeline gasped, fine brows arching above wide-spaced eyes so darkly circled by thick black lashes.

'With a grapevine like we have here?' her friend scoffed. 'I could probably describe him better than you could do yourself! A Linburgh, no less,' she went on mockingly. 'The name legends are made of. You do move in exclusive circles these days, Madeline.

'Don't I just?' she agreed, then added on a burst of inspiration. 'Hey—why don't you come to lunch here on Sunday! You could meet Perry yourself then, and maybe give your honest opinion of the real thing rather than the legend!'

The suggestion met with utter silence. A sudden tension buzzing so strongly down the line that it was impossible to miss it, though she did not understand the reason for it.

'I'm afraid I can't do that,' she heard Vicky say coolly.

'Why?' She frowned. 'Got a date?'

There was another small silence, then, 'Don't you know, Madeline?' Vicky asked curiously.

'Know what?' Her tone alone said she had no idea what Vicky was referring to.

The other girl sighed, muttered something not very ladylike which had Madeline's eyebrows arching all over again, then lowering into an incredulous frown as Vicky curtly explained, 'The Gilburns and the Stantons no longer acknowledge each other, dear,' she was informed with a shivering derision. 'They haven't since you and my brother split up.'

Louise walked into the room just as Madeline was slowly replacing the telephone receiver.

'Your young man, dear?' she enquired.

'No.' Madeline was still frowning. 'Vicky,' she said grimly, then looked up at Louise. 'Is it true?' she demanded. 'Have our two families been involved in a feud for the last four years?'

'Oh, dear,' Louise sighed and sat down next to Madeline on the sofa. 'I wondered how soon you would find out.'

Horrified, Madeline jerked to her feet. 'I can't believe it!' she exclaimed.

'No, neither could I when it first began,' Louise agreed. 'Men are such children sometimes, Madeline!' she sighed. 'And I've been warning your father for weeks that he ought to put a stop to it before you came home. But he refuses to listen. He blames James Stanton for starting it—after Dominic, of course, that is—and I can only assume that James blames your father—after you. Am I being too honest, Madeline?' she broke off to ask anxiously when she saw Madeline's face grow steadily more distressed as she went on. 'I have no wish to upset you with all of this, but it is a problem which has to be taken note of simply because you will sense it the moment we all get together in the same room.'

'Oh, so you do actually move in the same company,' Madeline scowled. 'I suppose that has to mean something.'

'Not much,' Louise grunted. 'We may attend the same things but we never acknowledge one another.'

'Good grief!' Madeline exploded. 'But that's positively—archaic!'

'I entirely agree with you, dear.' Louise nodded. 'But it's there and has to be faced. And I wouldn't like you to make some terrible gaffe by speaking to the Stantons this Saturday night at the Lassiters' only to find yourself cut dead where you stand.'

'Y-you mean, they would actually do that?' Her blue eyes widened in pained disbelief. 'No wonder Vicky was so damned touchy whenever we mentioned family! My God,' she breathed, utterly appalled by it all.

'Your father felt sure you would be able to cope,' Louise was looking pensive at Madeline's paste-white face, 'but if you don't feel you can face it all just yet, Madeline, we would understand if you preferred not to attend . . .'

'Oh, I'm going,' Madeline murmured ominously. 'And don't think for one moment that I shall be joining in your petty feud!'

'I thought you might say that,' Louise grimaced.

Another sudden thought brought Madeline's gaze arrowing on to her stepmother. 'Does this also mean that the Stantons have not been invited to Nina's wedding?' she demanded, saw the answer in Louise's uncomfortable face and was furious. 'Vicky is my best friend!' she cried. 'We—all three of us—Nina, Vicky and I planned to be bridesmaids at each other's wedding!

Are you now telling me that even poor Vicky has been
made a pariah by this family?'

'I'm so sorry, dear.'

'I should hope you jolly well are!' Madeline snapped,
so angry her eyes were flashing in a way that they hadn't
done once since she'd returned home. 'For the first time,
I feel heartily glad that I've come back! It's time it
stopped, Louise,' she stated grimly. 'And you can tell
Daddy that I'm going to see to it that it does!'

'You can tell him that yourself, Madeline,' Louise drily
declined the offer as she came gracefully to her feet. 'The
subject has been made taboo between your father and
me ever since we fell out over it for a whole month! I
don't ever intend to put myself through that kind of pur-
gatory again.' She shuddered at the mere memory of it.
'No,' she reached up to pat Madeline's shoulder, 'any
sorting of this problem will have to come from you,
darling, since you're the one who is at the root of it.'

And Dominic, Madeline added crossly to herself as
Louise left her to seethe alone. How could he have allowed things to deteriorate into this state? And how
darned petty!

She needed to talk to Vicky, she decided. And urgently if something wasn't to be done before Nina's
wedding-day. Grimly, she picked up the phone and
dialled the Stanton home number, crossing her fingers
that she would catch Vicky before she left for the day.

She did just. 'I've changed my mind about today,' she
told her friend. 'What time do you usually have lunch?'

Loath though she was to admit it, it was with great reluctance that Madeline rode the Stanton Bank lift to the
executive floor later that morning.

On the face of it, meeting Vicky at her place of work
had seemed logical since it was Madeline who was flexible

with her time and Vicky restricted by what might require attention on her desk. But even with the assurance that both Vicky's father and Dominic were to be out of the building all day today, she was still finding it difficult to be here, in the enemy camp so to speak, she thought with feudal dryness.

Still. At least she knew she looked good. Her taupe jacquard suit was elegant, and reacted well with the deep purple accessories she'd teamed with it. Her hair was plaited in a single thick braid down her back, and her newly acquired self-awareness—forced on her by her mother—helped her maintain an air of cool self-possession—even if it didn't go more than skin-deep.

Four years ago she wouldn't have given a second thought to how others might see her. She had used to wear what she enjoyed wearing rather than what was considered appropriate for the occasion—but then, she mused rather heavily, she had used to laugh infectiously when she thought something funny, cry real tears at the drop of a hat! The old Madeline had flitted her way through life on a restless ever-changing spirit. This new one tempered every move and gesture to suit the status quo.

Her composure was now inscrutable, her sophistication an indisputable fact. She walked, talked, behaved as the daughter of a prominent man of the City should do. She never revealed ruffled nerves, wouldn't dream of putting on a show of temperament like the old Madeline had used to do often—and to her ruin, she reminded herself. Her dress sense was superb, her personal grooming impeccable, and her manner serene. And if those closest to her were surprised to the point of dismay in the change in her, they had to agree, surely, that this new Madeline was far more acceptable than the old one?

That wretched girl who had run away four years ago was now back, and determined to make a point. She had begun with her family, and intended continuing by facing the people who had hurt her the most. The Stantons mainly, bar Vicky, and really only one Stanton in particular who was going to be made to eat those bitter words he'd thrown at her four years ago—even if he had set her off balance slightly with their unexpected meeting last night.

And she intended to do it by calmly smoothing out the quarrel between their two families. How, she wasn't sure yet. She only knew that she was going to do it, and show them all that Madeline Gilburn had matured into a cool sensible woman at last.

The lift doors slid open, and she stepped gracefully out into the luxurious foyer of the Stanton directors' floor, pausing for only a moment to collect herself as old memories hit out at her senses.

Once upon a time, she had rode that lift and bounced out here like an inmate, blithely trotting past the disgruntled receptionist of the day to walk right into Dominic's office without knocking—just so she could surprise him with a kiss before walking blithely out again!

Now she cringed at the very idea of doing such a thing. So gauche—so adolescent.

The walls of panelled walnut still looked the same, and the same deep-pile grey Wilton carpet still covered the floor. Everything, in fact, was just as she remembered it—except the smiling face of the receptionist already on her feet and waiting to greet her.

Madeline flicked a brief glance at the several closed doors she knew led to the plush offices of the individual Stanton Bank directors, James Stanton's dead centre, Dominic to the right of his and the rest belonging to lesser members of powerful family. She had no idea which door belonged to Vicky. Four years ago, the family had been dismayed at their daughter's desire to join the firm. Now things were different. Vicky would be different, Madeline reminded herself. She too was older, would be more self-assured now that she held a responsible position in the bank.

'Miss Stanton is expecting me,' Madeline informed the waiting receptionist. 'I'm Madeline Gilburn.'

The woman's smile warmed into rueful humour. 'She's been jumping about like a demented flea all morning because you were coming. If you'll just take a seat for a moment, I'll put her out of her misery and let her know you've arrived.'

But the receptionist didn't get the chance to inform Vicky of anything, because just at that moment a door further along the row flew open and out bounced Victoria Stanton—who came to a jerking halt when she saw Madeline standing there.

Grey eyes so like her brother's gazed at her transfixed, thickening Madeline's throat with tears as she stared into the pretty diminutive face of her closest friend. She had been wrong about Vicky, she acknowledged tearfully. She hadn't changed, not one single iota.

'Maddie——!' she cried, coming back to life with a stunned blinking of her eyes. 'Good God,' she gasped. 'It is you, isn't it?' then, before Madeline had a chance to say anything at all, Vicky was rushing across the room to fling herself into her arms. 'Oh, you beautiful, beautiful creature! I have missed you so!' She pressed a satisfying kiss on Madeline's cheek, then leaned back to stare at her again. 'Goodness me, but you've changed,' she told her. 'You look so—so . . .'

'Grown-up?' Madeline solemnly supplied when at last Vicky floundered. 'You too,' she smiled. 'You look quite the hot-shot executive in that pin-striped suit!

'It comes with the job,' Vicky explained the severe
tailoring of the suit which accentuated every nuance of
her hour-glass figure. 'Specially made for bottom-
wiggling at the——'

'Judith, have you heard from——?'

Silence fell like a stone. Vicky's excitement switched
off like a light as she spun round to stare in horror at
her brother while he fixed his narrowed gaze on her best
friend.

The very air in the foyer began to tingle. And so did
Madeline's senses as she stared at him without even
managing to breathe.

Meeting Dominic on a dark moonlit night bore no
resemblance to meeting him like this, in broad daylight,
where there was nothing—nothing to help mute the effect
he had upon her senses.

Four years, she thought desperately, four years of
quelling the aches, sealing up the wounds, learning to
come to terms with the public rejection and humiliation
he had forced on her, and it had all been for nothing.
She had suspected it last night when he had caught her
so unawares. But it was only now, as she stood face to
face with him in the cruel light of day, that she had to
accept that no amount of self-discipline was ever going
to erase the profound effect he'd always had on her. And
all she could think, and bitterly at that, was—thank God
for Boston! Because she knew that, whatever turmoil
was wringing at her insides, her face remained su-
premely calm and composed.

'Hello, Dominic,' she greeted quietly, accepting that
it was for her to break the silence since nobody else
seemed capable of it. 'You're looking—well.'

'Madeline,' he acknowledged huskily, running his
narrowed gaze over her as if he couldn't believe what he
was seeing. 'And you,' he returned equably. 'Very dif-

ferent, in fact,' he added on a note which told her he was talking about last night, not four years ago.

'M-Maddie is taking me out to lunch!' Vicky put in with a voice so high-pitched that it hovered just this side of hysterical. Then her poor friend began talking quickly, saying things that no one else listened to. Even Judith, the receptionist, was too busy flicking her eyes from Dominic's face to Madeline's in wide-eyed curiosity to hear a word Vicky said.

'You've not returned to Boston yet, then,' Dominic drawled across his sister's nervous chatter.

Instantly recognising the dig, she moved her chin upwards in mild defiance. 'Since I only arrived home yesterday, I'm not likely to be rushing straight back, am I? Though,' she added exclusively for his benefit, 'once England begins to pall, no doubt I shall go back—home.'

In his turn, Dominic did not miss her own subtle meaning in the final word. And his mouth tightened on it.

'I th-thought you were out today,' Vicky rushed in agitatedly. 'Y-you said you were—all day—out at some meeting.'

'I changed my mind,' Dominic informed Vicky while not removing his eyes from Madeline. 'And aren't I glad I did?' he added silkily. 'A Gilburn in our bank again; quite a surprise, Vicky. How did you manage to do it?'

It was time to put a stop to this, Madeline decided angrily as she saw Vicky's hands clench convulsively at her stomach. It was one thing him wishing to mock her, but quite another to use his sister as a tool to do it with.

With a slight lifting of her chin, she held Dominic's gaze for a short second which felt more like an hour in the throbbing tension, then slowly closed her dark lashes over her eyes. When she opened them again, she was looking directly at Vicky. 'We'll lose our table if you don't hurry,' she reminded her friend softly.

With a silent 'O' formed by two Cupid's bow lips and a pair of rounded eyes which showed a horrified appreciation of the way Madeline had just discarded her brother, Vicky turned and shot back into her office. She must have dived for her bag, because she was back with them before anyone had a chance to move.

With all the cool aplomb her mother had instilled into her, Madeline smiled pleasantly at the hovering receptionist, sent Dominic a cool nod, then was turning towards the lift, ignoring the hot needles of fury that impaled her as she went, chatting lightly to a wholly absorbed Vicky.

'God in heaven!' Vicky literally wilted against the panelled lift wall. 'That was just awful!'

'Not—pleasant,' Madeline drily agreed.

'He's an arrogant swine!' Dominic's sister ground out. 'Sometimes I——'

'He was taken by surprise, that's all,' Madeline put in, surprised by her instant rise to Dominic's defence.

'Taken by surprise, my foot!' scoffed Vicky. 'He knew damned well that you were coming here today—I told him! Made him promise to stay out of the way! God,' she choked, 'I could kill him for doing that, the rotten devil!'

The lunch was not the resounding success it should have been. Madeline's confrontation with Dominic had helped spoil it, but it was the feud between their two families which completely ruined the day.

'It's crazy,' Vicky agreed. 'They don't seem to mind that you and I stay friends. But my father will have nothing to do with yours, and vice versa.' She grimaced, 'It's made the last four years damned difficult for me if you must know. I daren't speak to your family because it would upset my lot, but I can't just snub people who have always been warm and caring towards me. So I stay out of the local social scene for most of the time. That way I don't get pulled in two different directions.'

'Is there no way you can think of that would put an end to it?' Madeline asked anxiously.

Vicky lifted her face and smiled rather cynically. 'Not unless you and Dominic fancy getting back together again—— No,' she then said quickly when Madeline stiffened up. 'I didn't mean that seriously. It's just that...' She sighed, frowning. 'He was sorry afterwards you know. He tried to see you, but...'

'I don't wish to know.' Had he? Had he tried to see her? she wondered. He can't have tried very hard, then, she stubbornly dismissed the weak sensation Vicky's claim touched her with.

'He was appalled at himself. He...'

'Vicky!' she warned.

'All right—all right.' The other girl waved a placatory hand. 'I just wanted to understand, that's all. I never did. Nobody did.'

'It was no one else's business.' Madeline flatly pointed out. 'Yet they all made it their business by starting this silly feud!' she added impatiently.

'They all hurt for their respective chicks, Madeline; surely you can understand that? When you went off to Boston you left one big hornets' nest of bottled-up emotion behind you. Even Dominic shot off out of it to our sister bank in Australia for six months. By the time he got back, they'd quarrelled so badly that nothing was going to shift either your father or mine.'

'Did he try?' Madeline asked wryly.

'Of course he tried!' Vicky bristled instantly in her brother's defence. 'We all tried! Even the timid Nina, for all the good it did her,' she muttered.

'How?' Madeline asked, surprised to hear that Nina could even find the courage to intervene in any dispute—she had used to run out of the room when Madeline had one of her spats with her father.

'She insisted we be invited to her wedding,' Vicky said. 'Apparently, your father said he was quite happy to see me walk behind Nina down the aisle as one of her bridesmaids—but the rest of 'em could go to hell!' Vicky's gruff mimic of her father's rasping voice was very good, but while doing it she also revealed her own disgust.

'And Nina actually told you that?' She was beginning to wonder if her stepsister had changed beyond all recognition if she could repeat something as cruel as that to Vicky.

'Of course she didn't!' Vicky denied, to Madeline's relief. 'Annie, your housekeeper, told Clara, our housekeeper, and she was so affronted on our behalf that she told us.'

'And the feud worsened,' Madeline added heavily. 'God, what a mess.'

'Anyway, it was all so much hot air over nothing,' Vicky finished grimly. 'Because there was no way I was going to be able to be bridesmaid at Nina's wedding while my own family remained in exile.'

It was a mess, and one Madeline saw no way out of. She left Vicky feeling as dissatisfied with their meeting as she had been with anything for a long time. It seemed so damned unfair that Vicky, the innocent in all of it, should be the one to lose out! She wanted Vicky at Nina's wedding, but she had backed off from inviting her personally, because of the strain she saw it would place on Vicky's loyalty to her own family. To attend without them would be disloyal. Yet her not being there seemed equally disloyal to her friendship with Madeline.

It was a dilemma, and one Madeline saw no answer to as she went home that afternoon. And for the first time, she seriously considered calling Dominic to see if he could come up with a solution.

So she wasn't so surprised when he took it upon himself to ring her instead.

CHAPTER FOUR

'WE HAVE to talk. Have dinner with me.'

'W-what did you say?' The sound of his voice, washing deep and seductively over her via the telephone earpiece, was enough on its own to make her deaf to the words he actually said.

'Have dinner with me,' he repeated huskily. And her throat closed up on a wave of nostalgia those few gruff words resurrected from years ago when he had asked her the selfsame question in the exact same intimate tone. Was it done deliberately? She couldn't tell. 'We must talk.'

'How dare you ring me here!' she whispered, glancing furtively around the empty hallway, She was alone, thank God! But it was only by fluke that she had happened to answer the phone because she was expecting a call from Perry.

'Why, will your father beat you if he finds out you've been talking to me?' he drawled.

'Probably,' she grimaced, remembering the stand-up row she'd had with her father over the Stanton affair. It hadn't got her anywhere, and she was beginning to realise just how impossible the situation had become.

'He wouldn't harm a hair on your lovely head, and you know it,' came the sardonic reply. 'Now, about dinner.'

'I can't,' she answered bluntly, searching her mind for an adequate excuse why not, then realising that she didn't need one when the truth was clear enough. 'I don't want to, actually.'

'Actually,' he mocked, 'I don't think either of us has much choice. Not if you don't want to see Vicky hurt more than she has been already over this damned wedding of Nina's.'

'All right, I accept that something has to be done and perhaps you and I are the only ones to do it,' she agreed. 'But I am not prepared to share another slanging match with you, Dominic,' she warned him coolly.

'No?' he murmured provocatively. 'What a shame. We used to have such fun throwing insults at each other...'

'Well, not any more,' she said coldly, hurt that he could be so cruel as to taunt her about their row four years ago.

'So, when can we meet?' he enquired more briskly, obviously deciding he had provoked her enough for one day.

Not at all if I had any choice, Madeline thought heavily. 'Not before next week,' she told him out loud. 'Today is Friday, and my weekend is fully booked.'

'The Lassiter thing?'

'Yes,' she said. 'The Lassiter thing.'

'We could meet there,' he suggested. 'You know, sneak off somewhere to some secret location and have a little pow-wow all on our own...?'

Madeline closed her eyes, her pulses automatically beginning to race as a trace of the old Madeline fondness for intrigue pierced its way through her armour. Was that why he'd made that outrageous suggestion, she wondered agitatedly, because he knew it would appeal to her old wayward nature?

But not her new careful nature it didn't. So, 'Sorry,' she drawled. 'But my—partner wouldn't like me sneaking off like that.'

'Partner?' Madeline had the satisfaction of hearing his voice sharpen. 'What partner?'

'The one I brought with me from Boston,' she informed him coolly. 'Perry Linburgh.'

'Ah,' he breathed, pretending no knowledge of Perry when she was sure as dammit that if Vicky knew about Perry, then Dominic surely did. 'Byron Linburgh's son and heir.' He sounded suitably impressed. 'My, but we do move in exalted circles, do we not?'

'Thank you.' She refused to take up the bait, and Dominic's own short sigh of acknowledgement to that whispered down the line to shiver right through her.

'Dinner next week, then,' he said, dropping the sarcasm.

'Not dinner, no,' she refused. 'I don't think it——'

'Lunch, then, in London,' he cut in.

'No.' Madeline bit down on her bottom lip. 'Dominic, I——'

'A drink,' he thrust curtly at her. 'Meet me for a drink in Newbury one evening, and we'll...'

'Dominic,' she broke in gently, softening her tone because in this particular case she had no wish to wound him. 'You just have to understand that I can't afford to be seen anywhere alone with you. The cost will run too high.'

'What cost?' His anger whipped at her, and Madeline flinched, accepting his right to it. 'What's wrong with being seen with me? I don't have some dreaded social disease, you know.'

'I never meant to imply that you——'

'Look——' he bit out tightly, then heaved in a deep breath to control the sudden flare of temper. 'You'll meet me, Madeline, out in the open, and for dinner one evening, or I come around to your home to see you tonight. Which will it be?' he asked tightly. 'A civilised dinner for two, or a very uncivilised confrontation at your home with your damned family as witness!'

'Dinner, then,' she reluctantly agreed, not even bothering to call his bluff. Dominic was quite capable of carrying out any threat he uttered.

'Where?' He shot the question at her like a bullet.

'In Newbury—— No.' That was too close to home. 'I have to be in London on Wednesday next week.' For gown fittings with Nina. It should be easy enough to find a convincing excuse why she couldn't come back home with Nina in the evening. Nina had a function to attend with Charles that night, so there should be no chance of her stepsister deciding to stay in the City with her. 'At least there we have less of a chance of being recognised,' she added drily.

'I am quite prepared to meet you anywhere and in front of anyone, Madeline,' he said grimly. 'Since when have you become so damned protective of your so-called reputation?'

'My father would tell you, Dominic, that for all my sins I only needed teaching a lesson once before it sank indelibly in.'

'He might, if he was speaking to me,' he ruefully agreed. 'But since he isn't—and hasn't for four years— it seems pointless to remark upon it, don't you think?'

Perry arrived on Saturday in a dashing red Lotus sports car. Madeline met him in the driveway with a warm hug.

'That was nice,' he murmured, smiling down at her. 'But I wonder why there was a hint of desperation about it?'

'Oh...' She shook her dark head. 'It's all been a bit of a strain here, that's all,' she dismissed, turning within the curve of his arm to walk with him into the house.

'I'm still feeling like a visitor after being away for so long.'

'Good,' he said. 'Keep feeling like that. Then perhaps you won't be tempted to stay too long before coming home to us in Boston.'

'Why?' she murmured provocatively. 'Will you miss me when you have to go back?'

'You know I will.' He squeezed her closer to him. 'If I have to return without you,' he then added meaningfully.

'And what about the lovely Christina?' she reminded him. 'I'm sure she won't like you arriving back in Boston with me on your arm.'

'Christina knows how I feel,' he stated coolly. But Madeline wasn't fooled in the slightest by his offhand reply.

Madeline was quite aware that Perry used her as protection against the beautiful but very spoiled Christina van Neilson. One of the reasons why she and Perry had gravitated towards each other in the first place was because they were both hiding a broken heart, and recognised the struggle in each other. Madeline didn't like the Boston beauty, but she could understand why Perry did. Christina was probably the closest you could get to American royalty, a tall willowy golden beauty with the van Neilson billions to give her everything she wanted in her over-indulged life.

She wanted Perry, royalty himself if it was wealth that made the distinction. But she wanted him on her own terms—and those terms did not include Perry working for his living when she wanted to play. Christina had been a fool when she challenged that inbred sense of responsibility Perry possessed with her 'get out from under the family wing and live the kind of jet-setting life I'm used to, or no Christina' ultimatum. It was no contest. Christina had lost, but at the expense of poor Perry's heart.

Whether or not the beauty's own heart was involved was difficult to say with someone as superficial as Christina. She certainly did not like the closeness there was between Madeline and Perry. But that could just be spoiled possessiveness.

'Forman didn't take up my father's invitation to come with you, then,' she noted, wisely changing the subject.

'He's in Brussels,' Perry informed her. 'Maybe I can talk him into coming next weekend.'

'That would be nice,' she murmured casually.

'Why?' He glanced frowningly at her. 'You aren't fancying him, are you?'

Madeline laughed. 'He's not my type,' she assured him. 'Too big and brooding for my taste. I'll stick to you if you don't mind.'

'I don't mind in the least,' he grinned, dropping a light kiss upon her cheek, 'but watch it, if Forman does come,' he warned. 'A real rake if I ever knew one.'

'Has a way with the ladies, does he?' she murmured curiously.

'Makes me jumpy just to have him around,' Perry mocked. 'Safety in numbers is Forman's motto, and my God, does he live by it!'

Madeline just laughed again, and took him in to meet her family. By the time he had spent an hour talking City business with her father, complimented Louise on her lovely home, and gently teased Nina into blushing, her family were ready to announce Perry great!

She dressed with a care that told her just how apprehensive she was about this first airing of the new Madeline in Lambourn society. Four years ago she had made a public clown of herself, and most of the people present tonight would have been present that night too.

It was that last humiliating appearance they would have carried around in their memories ever since. Which meant this appearance had to so overshadow it that would only see this one—and not the clown.

So instead of the palest lime silk she had worn to her downfall, she wore black. Dramatic-lined, simple sheathed matt black. The fine silk crêpe had been exclusively designed for her to follow each subtle line of her tall and slender shape. It covered her from throat to wrist to ankle, its only adornment a wine-red silk cord circling her narrow waist and tied loosely so it draped her slender hips to hang low on the flat of her stomach. Severely gothic in style, the skirt fluted very slightly from the knees to swirl gently around her ankles.

She clipped dark rubies to her wrists and ears, added a matching choker to her throat—the whole set a present from her mother and Lincoln for her twenty-first birthday.

She slipped her feet into high black satin mules then turned to view the finished affect in the long dressing mirror. Her hair she had swept up into a simple knot to leave her creamy neck exposed for her glinting rubies. Her make-up had been applied to add drama to her eyes and mouth, the long thickness of her lashes a lush frame to the vivid blue of her eyes, mouth the same dark red as the rubies. Studying herself, Madeline saw what she wanted to see, the complete antithesis of that other frilled and flounced girl they would remember. And with herself alone knowing how much nervousness she was suffering inside, she turned and left her room.

'Goodness me!' her father exclaimed as she entered the drawing-room to find them all waiting for her. 'Is that really my girl?' He brought all the other heads swinging around to stare at her in several expressions of amazement. Except Perry, dear Perry who only knew this elegantly sophisticated creature and could not understand everyone else's awe.

'Perfect, darling.' He came towards her with a smile which said how lovely he found her. 'Dee would be proud of you tonight if she could see you.'

'Thank you,' she murmured softly. Uncanny though it was, Perry always knew exactly what to say to her to put her at ease. The agitated flutters in her stomach eased and her pulses calmed. 'Quite the handsome beau yourself tonight, Perry,' she returned.

'Thank you, ma'am.' He offered her a mocking bow, looking very attractive in his black dinner suit, his hazelnut eyes twinkling at her.

Despite her confidence that she'd hidden it well, her family must have all known how nervous she felt, Madeline acknowledged hours later when the Lassiter party was in full swing and she was at last beginning to relax—mainly because there was no sign of a single Stanton in evidence.

'They love you dearly, don't they?' Perry remarked at her side. She turned to look at him to find him studying her gravely. 'You have a wonderful family, Madeline. Each one of them—including your future brother-in-law—have taken it in turns to stay close by your side... Why is that, I wonder?' His gaze left her studiedly bland face to wander slowly around the crowded room. 'There isn't a person here tonight who hasn't at some point or another stood staring at you in disbelief.' That shrewd gaze came back to her. 'And again, I wonder why I get the feeling that they see you as some very unpredictable explosive substance they just daren't trust, no matter how utterly serene you look.' Hazel eyes studied her narrowly. 'I've heard the Stanton name bandied about like crazy,' he went on, 'picked up on little remarks about Boston and the changes it has wreaked. I have even overheard my own name being bantered about with a kind of delicious awe, and seriously wondered if the tension sizzling in this place tonight is actually going to catch fire... Why, I again wonder?' His hand came up to lightly brush the satin smoothness of her cheek. 'Was *he* supposed to be present here tonight, darling,' he murmured huskily, 'the man you were once engaged to?'

It was her turn to let her gaze drift around the Lassiters' packed drawing-room. 'The Stantons had a— prior engagement, it seems, that they could not get out of,' she told him with only the slightest hint of cynicism for the effect that excuse had on her. Looking back at him, she added drily, 'Dominic Stanton and I did not part gracefully, I suppose you could say.'

'You were engaged to Dominic Stanton?' His surprise made her smile, and her mocking nod made his fair brows arch. 'I never did ask you his name, did I?' he murmured ruefully.

'I suppose I should have warned you what to expect here tonight, but...' Her sigh was heavy. 'I think to have explained it all to you would have been like having to admit to myself that the nightmare I created four years ago actually existed, and I was still hoping, right up until we arrived here, that it was all just my own silly imagination.'

'You caused something of a scene?' he suggested shrewdly.

'What would probably best be described as a hum-dinger of one,' Madeline drily admitted. 'Since then our two families have not been on the best of terms.'

'And have all these people come here tonight expecting the Stantons to show up also?'

'What do you think?' she drawled.

'I think,' he said grimly, 'the place is full of bitches—men and women alike.'

Madeline just smiled. 'You won't believe it, Perry, but they have a right to expect trouble when I'm around. And to be fair to the Stantons,' she added quietly, 'their absence will not be meant as a slight to me, but their way of defusing a potentially awkward situation.'

'I've met him, you know,' Perry said suddenly, studying her look of wary surprise. 'Once and only briefly, the other day at a bank meeting I attended. He seems quite a man.'

'Dominic always was the dynamic businessman,' Madeline oh, so drily agreed.

'I was not referring to his business acumen, darling,' Perry drawled.

'No?' she mocked, not taking him on.

'No,' he said, and laughed because he knew that expression of old. 'There's music in the other room. Let's go and dance.'

'What a lovely idea!' she cried, allowing him to take her arm. 'You know,' she drawled, 'I could become a trifle bored with this provincial crowd if I stay around them too long.'

'That's my girl.' He patted her hand where it lay in the crook of his arm. 'Show them all how truly sophisticated you are.'

'You see too much,' she grumbled.

'And you, my darling Madeline, hide too much.'

'I promise to tell all later,' she vowed as she went into his arms for the dance.

'I'll keep you to that,' he warned.

And he did, once they were back home and left alone after everyone else had gone off to bed. Madeline sighed, wondered where to start, then decided the beginning was the only sensible place, which was exactly where she began, leaving hardly anything out, and by the time her voice faltered to a husky halt Perry's face had gone pale with anger.

'The bastard!' he rasped.

'No,' Madeline wearily protested. 'Believe me, Perry, when I tell you that I deserved all I got.' She dragged in a deep breath then let it out again. 'You can't begin to know the kind of person I was then. So spoiled, so criminally wilful! I must have driven Dominic to the point of insanity several times before he eventually snapped. I was an absolute terror. There was no controlling me once I got an idea into my head. I was a danger to myself—and to those people around me. I don't blame Dominic for what he did to me that night— God knows,' she sighed, 'I'd had it coming. I just—just wish he'd found a kinder way of putting me in my place, that's all.'

'Rubbish!' Perry dismissed. 'You were young and foolhardly, but that gave him no excuse to humiliate you in that brutal way!'

How could Perry be expected to understand things as they had been then when he could only see the new cool and self-disciplined Madeline? she wondered heavily as she lay awake in bed later than night. Even that tiny hint of impishness at the Lassisters' had stunned him, he was so unused to seeing it. A headstrong and ungovernable Madeline was quite beyond his comprehension.

Nor had she told him about the less obvious pressures brought to bear upon herself and Dominic. From the moment they had shown an interest in each other, they had been picked up and carried along by their families' mutual enthusiasm for a match.

It had felt as if they were under constant surveillance from both family and friends. Everywhere they went there had always seemed to be someone more than willing to monitor their every move and gesture towards one another, eager to encourage, to tease, to automatically assume that if they were together they had to be in love—which, Madeline had to admit, she'd thought too at the time.

They had been engaged within a month of their first dinner date, and there was hardly a person living in Lambourn who hadn't wanted to celebrate it with them in some way or another. So much so that she and Dominic had hardly ever found time to be on their own.

Maybe if they had been left alone to allow the relationship to develop at its own pace things would not have got so out of hand. But as it was, and like everything else to do with the old Madeline, she had thrown herself into the excitement of it all as eagerly as everyone else had. Only Dominic had remained calm and unaffected throughout it all. He had seemed more amused by her than anything else, quite happy to indulge her crazy love of secret assignations, meeting her down by the river somewhere for a private hour or so of gentle lovemaking, willing to tease her, play with her emotions with light kisses and mild petting, but any sign of things flaring out of control and he had been quick to curtail things, leaving her feeling only more restless and frustrated as the weeks went by.

She had known he wanted her—she wasn't so innocent that she didn't known what desire looked like when it glowed in a man's eyes—but his self-control had infuriated her, so, in typical Madeline style, she had gone all out to seduce him, and Dominic, though slowly beginning to reveal cracks in his impressive control, had continued to resist her every lure until the tension growing between them had meant they started to argue more than kiss, and she'd harboured a suspicion that Dominic had actually been relieved when he'd had to go away on a week-long business trip to Bonn.

The night he had been due back was also the same night the whole family were supposed to be going to see the latest musical block-buster currently playing in the West End. And Madeline had found herself in the rare position of having Dominic all to herself for a whole evening.

Dominic had arrived at the house, dressed in casual jeans and a pale blue shirt, ready to spend a rare evening alone with his fiancée. And had found a surprise waiting for him....

CHAPTER FIVE

'WHAT the hell are you playing at coming to the door dressed like that?' Dominic's rasping bark came rattling down the years to make Madeline wince even now, four years on. He had stared at her as if he couldn't believe his eyes.

'Don't you like it?' Wearing her father's best dress shirt—and nothing else bar the flimsiest pair of lacy briefs—she'd thought then that she looked far more seductive than any Mata Hari could do. But, looking back now, she could only cringe in horror now at her own brazenness. It was no wonder Dominic was appalled at her.

'Go and get some clothes on,' he commanded, thrusting her ungently inside so that he could close the front door.

Instead, she moved in close to wind her arms around his neck, 'Without even a kiss from my loving fiancé?' She widened her deep blue eyes at him, seducing him with every lure she possessed.

'Madeline . . .'

'It's all right,' she murmured huskily, 'we're completely alone,' and stopped his protests with her mouth, taking the initiative and kissing him with a hunger that had been building steadily over the weeks. He returned the kiss with an angry reluctance that made him growl, but he parted her lips so that he could deepen the kiss himself. She could still recall the heat of his body as she pressed against him, and the quivering rush of excitement that flooded through her as his arms came wrapping convulsively around her. It was her first real experience of sexual ignition, a lightning that sparked into a flame that began to lick right through her. And her body melted against him, her need so strong that it blanked out everything else.

He picked her up in his arms, and she clung to him, her mouth refusing to let his go as he carried her up the stairs. The pounding of his heart against her breast, the gasping sound of his laboured breathing, the fiery touch of his hands where he held her cradled to him, all culminated to make her unprepared for what Dominic really intended.

She was so drunk on her own success at getting him this far that she never even noticed his own lack of response to everything but the kiss. While her hands ran urgently over his shoulders and his back, revelling in the rippling muscle beneath her fingers, Dominic was grimly planning her punishment.

They reached her room. He sat down on her bed with her still cradled in his arms—and the next moment, he had flipped her over and was issuing her with her very first and only bottom-beating of her entire life!

Deaf to her cries of outrage, he delivered his punishment quite ruthlessly before tossing her off his lap on to the bed so he could get up and stride angrily for the door.

'You've been asking for that for years,' he growled as he turned to glare at her. 'You are a totally unprincipled, ungovernable brat, Madeline!' he snapped. 'And I'm beginning to wonder if I've gone mad wanting to marry myself to a sex-crazed little minx like you!'

Sex-crazed! 'I wouldn't marry you if you were the last man on earth!' she screamed at him, so wild with hurt and humiliation she could barely breathe. She knelt among the fluffy pink and white flowered duvet, her hair a mad tangle of black around her flushed face, eyes spitting a hatred at him that only made Dominic's mouth curl in deriding contempt. 'And you won't get another chance to lay a finger on me, you brute! I hate you, Dominic Stanton—I hate you!'

'You can come and apologise to me tomorrow,' he said, looking so incredibly aloof, so damned arrogantly pompous that her temper flew right out of control.

'I'll burn in hell first!' she vowed. And with a yank she dragged the lovely sapphire and diamond ring off her finger. 'I need a real man in my life,' she spat at him. 'Not some old has-been who's incapable of responding with any passion!'

The ring hit his back as he turned abruptly away from her. Now, on looking back on that awful scene, she could see that Dominic had been desperate to get away from the house before he retaliated to that unforgivable gibe. He had always been too sensitive to the gap in their ages, and, saying what she had, Madeline knew now that she had been lucky he hadn't jumped on her for a reply. As it was, the feel of something hitting his back brought him to a halt, and he turned slowly, looking down at the exquisite ring lying on the rose-pink carpet at his feet.

'I'm warning you, Madeline,' he said huskily as he lifted his grim gaze back to her. 'Stop right there before this gets entirely out of hand.'

Too furious to listen, too humiliated to care, and in the unusual position of being out of control of a situation, she couldn't stop the bitter words tumbling from her trembling lips. 'And I'm warning you,' she breathed. The sobs already racking her distraught frame, she delivered an ultimatum which really should have put an end to it all. 'You walk out of here now, and I shall have your replacement here before you even reach home!'

'Is that so?' he drawled, and suddenly she was afraid of him, cringing back against the pillows, thinking he was going to murder her by the look she saw glinting in those hard grey eyes. But all he did was bend and pick up the ring, then stand there twisting it thoughtfully between finger and thumb before glancing back at her. 'You know where to find me—and this, Madeline, when you're ready to apologise.' And he pocketed the ring and turned away.

'I mean it—*I mean it*!' she screamed at his retreating back.

'So do I,' she heard him mutter grimly as he disappeared from view.

As threatened, too proud to back down, and just too stupid to recognise when she was beaten, within the hour Madeline had the house full of friends, throwing herself into the gaiety of the party with an inflamed defiance spurring her on.

Perhaps, by morning, the bitter flames would have burned themselves out. Perhaps, if she'd been allowed to work off the terrible devils gnawing inside her, then she could have gone cap in hand to Dominic and begged forgiveness. But things didn't turn out that way. Instead, it was Dominic who took the initiative to return that night, Dominic who walked in to find the Gilburn house in the throes of a party even Madeline's long-suffering family would have been shocked by.

The front door was off the latch so Dominic only had to walk in, enter the dimly lit drawing-room where the reek of cigarette smoke and alcohol told its own story. He only had to flick on the overhead light and see a dozen or so bewildered faces turn his way, see Madeline stretched out on the sofa with the young man she had been dating before Dominic, her face flushed, her soft mouth swollen from another man's kisses, the incrimi-

nating shirt riding high on her silken thighs. His oddly
blank gaze remained fixed on her for a long nerve-
crackling moment, then he simply turned around and
walked right out of the house again.

She rushed after him, knowing with a cold feeling that
struck deep into the core of her that this time she had
sunk beyond redemption with this last defiance. She
caught him at his car, and it was there, in the quiet
darkness of the night, with the width of the black Ferrari
between them, that Dominic delivered the utter and
complete slaying of her character. He did it without pause
for breath, or by raising his voice beyond a harsh
whisper. And she received it all without offering a single
word in her own defence.

She had no defence. She had realised that even as she'd
run desperately after him. She knew it as she stood there
staring at his cold, contemptuous face and listened to
the words spilling out from his hard, ruthless lips.

By the time her family returned home, they found her
so sunk in misery that it took some urgent sleuthing to
find out what had happened.

Conscience alone would not allow her to leave things
there. She tried to ring him, only to be told he had gone
away again and wasn't expected back until the night of
the country club ball.

Within days, everyone in the area knew how Madeline
Gilburn had been caught red-handed by Dominic Stanton
in the arms of another man. The scandal was sen-
sational. She didn't dare go out of the house because of
the accusing looks she received. In everyone's eyes she
had, of course, run true to form and behaved appal-
lingly. And she suspected that most were pleased to have
their worst expectations about her confirmed.

'Wait until the ball; he'll be ready to listen then,' those who cared about her advised. 'He loves you, Madeline. Dominic will come around eventually.'

So she spent the following week living for the night of the ball, knowing Dominic would have to be there since his parents had taken on the task of organising it all this year.

Perhaps if Vicky had been home and able to talk some sense into her then she would not have walked herself right into her own public crucifixion. But Vicky was away at university—a thing Madeline had turned down when she fell in love with Dominic. So Vicky was blithely un-aware of the utter mess her best friend had made of her romance with her brother.

The night of the ball arrived, and Edward Gilburn worriedly watched his daughter as she came down the stairs towards him, dressed like a princess in a ballgown of the palest lime silk. Its fitted heart-shaped bodice curved the sensual swell of her breasts and nipped in to her narrow waist. And the full-length skirt was just a fine billow of layer upon layer of fine silk chiffon. She had left her hair down so it fell in glistening waves around her shoulders. She looked beautiful, frighteningly fragile, with no amount of make-up managing to hide the ravages of the last week. The only part of her seeming to be alive were her eyes, which glowed wide and dark in her pale face.

They arrived at the club to find they were one of the last to do so. And the first thing she saw was Dominic dancing with a beautiful blonde creature dressed in blood-red velvet.

Jealousy ripped through her. Nina's hand closing tightly on her own icy cold one made her aware of the avid looks she was receiving. The air was as tight as a drum, everyone expecting a spectacular Madeline

Gilburn scene, maliciously hoping she would run true to form and challenge Dominic right there in the ballroom.

'It's all right,' she murmured to Nina at her worried glance. 'I'm not going to do anything.'

And, to be fair, she didn't. Ignoring the tension which eddied around with her, she mingled with the crowd, chatted lightly, smiled a lot, and made a point of going to say hello to Dominic's parents, who were equally determined to pretend nothing untoward had happened. They welcomed her with hugs and kisses as they always did, and she stood beside them for several minutes talking about God knew what—she had an idea that even the Stantons didn't know what passed between them.

Slowly the room began to relax, and she continued to circulate with all the light-hearted innocençe of an unexploded bomb. All the time, her consciousness was fixed on Dominic—where he was, what he was doing—her heart beating hectically, her lungs aching with the effort it took to drag air past her constricted throat.

She was therefore limp with relief when after a dreadful hour of him completely ignoring her presence he came over to her and coolly drew her on to the dance-floor.

She went in his arms without a single word, mouth dry, eyes over-bright, skin tingling where his hands rested upon her.

'I am dancing with you only because my father requested I do it to avoid more scandal,' he informed her bluntly as he swung her away. 'So don't read anything into this which is not there.'

'I love you, Dominic,' she whispered huskily.

'You don't know the first meaning of the word!' he jeered. 'It's over between us, Madeline,' he informed her coldly, 'so just be a good girl for once in your

wretched life, and don't cause a scene—for our families'
sake if not for our own.'

'Won't you at least let me say I'm sorry?' she pleaded
with him, terrified at the look of granite-hard coldness
on his face. 'I think I went a little mad the other night,
I——'

'I don't wish to know,' he cut in. 'I find your juvenile
antics wearying to say the least. Stick to your own kind
from now on, Madeline, is my advice to you. Leave the
big boys alone and go and play with the young ones like
the one you were offering yourself to the other night.
They may fumble and have little finesse, but they'll give
you the quick kind of thrill that's all you seem to need
before moving on to the next experience, the next new
kick!'

'That's a terrible thing to say!' His revulsion at her
sent her emotions swinging into a violent downward
spiral, the bitter words thrashing against her wretched
senses as he twirled her around the dance-floor, his hand
biting into her as cruelly as his words were doing, re-
stricting her ability to breathe, think, to even notice the
tears filling her eyes.

'I didn't promise to be nice to you, Madeline,' he
gritted. 'Only to dance one damned dance with you!'

'Then let me go.' She tried to pull away from him, but
his grip only tightened. 'I don't need your benevolence.'

'Oh, no,' he refused through clenched white teeth.
'You'll stay right here and see this through! I've been
humiliated enough by you already!'

'And you didn't humiliate me the other night?' she
shot back, the tears gone now, replaced with an anger
that always came alongside pain for her.

'Because I wouldn't take what was so—cheaply offered?' he scoffed. 'Behave like a whore and you get
treated like one, Madeline. And you were playing the

whore to the bloody hilt! Don't!' he warned when her head came up, eyes like midnight fire in her paste-white face. 'Don't cause that scene, or you'll get more than you bargained for from me.'

'Revenge, Dominic?' she suggested shrilly. 'Is that what this is really all about: you want revenge on me, so you've decided to give me my one conciliatory dance then intend to walk away so everyone will know exactly why you danced with me at all!'

'That's your problem to deal with, Madeline, not mine,' he threw back carelessly. 'You could have stayed away tonight and saved us all this, but you didn't, so now you have the choice of either finishing it with a bit of class or doing what these people have come to expect from you, and showing yourself up for the crazy fool you really are!'

'Oh, by all means, let's not disappoint the punters by not giving them what they expect,' she drawled, her eyes brilliant with intent, heart cracking wide like an egg slowly seeping its dying contents. 'Now, what should it be, Dominic? Would you prefer me to dash out of here in a flood of tears, or would it be rather more amusing if I prostrate myself at your feet and humbly beg forgiveness?'

With a violent jerk, Madeline removed herself from his arms, and lifted her chin to send him a final glinting look from her pain-darkened eyes. 'I think the latter, don't you?' she murmured, and, with an odd twist spoiling the perfect contours of her mouth, she dropped into a low, deep and humbling curtsy at his feet, pale lime silk billowing around her, her gleaming black head bowed in mute contrition.

It was dramatic. It was utterly diabolical of her to do it. But as a country club ball stopper, it threw the whole room into total silence. And now, Madeline could ac-

tually find it in her to smile a little at her own wicked
temerity.

Dominic could have laughed, but he didn't. He could
have seen the humour in the precocious Madeline Gilburn
abasing herself in front of him like some lowly serf, but
he didn't. He could even have dragged her up by the hair
and given her another beating for causing the scene he
had specifically warned her against! But he did none of
these things. Instead, and on a filthy curse which only
reached as far as Madeline's ears, he derided, 'Why don't
you just grow up, Madeline? For God's sake grow up!'
and walked angrily away.

To everyone watching the little scene from the sidelines, they saw Dominic get his revenge that night, because Madeline's dramatic little gesture looked like a
desperate plea for forgiveness—not given. And in true
Madeline Gilburn style, she begged with optimum
impact—or that was how it appeared to the onlookers.
In truth—and as Dominic had known—she was mocking
him, and he walked away because he could see no other
way of dealing with the situation without appearing the
fool once again.

Madeline, by contrast, remained exactly where she
was, dying a little more with each second that passed,
taking with it all her brave defiance, her mind going over
and over every cruel word he had thrown at her, adding
them to the long list of criticisms he had hurled at her
the week before, and by the time her father gently lifted
her back to her feet and led her out of the room the old
Madeline was already dead, and the new one floun-
dering somewhere close to hell. It took six months in
Boston before the new woman began to form any real
substance, and years to build her into the person she
was today.

No one, Madeline had vowed often since, was going to find a single thing to criticise about her again.

She and Perry spent Sunday morning on horseback, riding across the lovely spring-green countryside to stop for lunch at a small riverside inn.

Afterwards, they went for a walk by the river, drawing the eyes of other Sunday strollers by the sheer balance one made against the other, Madeline long-legged and slender in her buff riding breeches and brown check tweed jacket, with her long hair caught up on a simple coil high on the crown of her head, and Perry dressed similarly, tall and lean, with his light brown hair and classically clean features.

They had been walking for a good ten minutes before Madeline plucked up enough courage to ask him the question which had been gnawing at her all weekend. 'Perry...' she murmured carefully. 'Can I ask a favour of you?'

'Of course,' he said agreeably. 'Anything you want.'

Just like that. Madeline smiled a little ruefully to herself. That was not going to be his attitude in a moment. 'If I tell my parents I am dining with you in London on Wednesday night, will you cover for me?'

He stopped walking. 'Why?' he demanded. 'Why do you need cover?'

Madeline ran her tongue around her suddenly dry lips. 'Because I've arranged to meet someone,' she explained. 'And they're going to disapprove thoroughly if they know who.'

'Who?'

Logical next question, she acknowledged. Oh, gosh! She took a deep breath. 'Dominic,' she said, then cringed when he turned angrily on her.

'Are you losing your mind?' he cried. 'The man virtually crucified you in public four years ago, and now you calmly tell me that you've arranged to have dinner with him!'

There was nothing calm about the decision, Madeline thought drily. 'I crucified him first, Perry,' she pointed out. 'This community is small and tightly knit. For as long as this stupid feud between our two families goes on, that dual crucifixion will never be forgotten. And it's hurting people who have no right to be hurt by it. I am meeting Dominic because we both accept that something has to be done to bring it all to an end, and it seems that we are the only ones who can do it.'

'How?' he jeered. 'By seeing each other again? Pretending the past never existed?'

'Yes,' she answered, then more fiercely, 'Yes! If that is what it takes!'

'Then you're a fool!' he muttered gruffly. 'Because the past did exist! And you've spent the last four years of your life recovering from the wounds it inflicted on you! He inflicted on you! For God's sake, woman,' he muttered harshly, 'see sense! Steer well clear of him. Protect yourself and let the rest of them sort themselves out!'

'I'm not intending jumping all over him, you know!' she said defensively. 'Just meeting him for dinner and discussing family problems!'

'How do you know?' he shot back. 'The way I read it, he led you around by the nose four years ago. What makes you think he won't have the same power over you now?'

That stung—mainly because it was so near to the truth—and forced her to respond accordingly. 'That's a bit like the pot calling the kettle black, isn't it?'

He had the grace to flush. 'All right. Point taken,' he grunted. Christina van Neilson had made a fool of him several times with other men before Perry had eventually snapped.

'But that doesn't answer my question,' he pointed out. 'You haven't so much as set eyes on him in four years, so how do you know how you're going to feel about him?'

Madeline lowered her face—but not quickly enough for Perry's sharp gaze. 'Ah,' he concluded tightly. 'So you have seen him.'

She didn't answer. It was too late anyway. Perry had already seen the truth written in her eyes. 'When?' he demanded gruffly. 'Where?'

'One evening,' she told him. 'When I was out riding and we happened to meet up.' She didn't tell him which night. She didn't dare.

'And what happened?'

'Oh, don't worry about it, Perry,' she mocked the sudden concern in his eyes. 'We picked up from where we left off four years ago—throwing insults at each other.' She smiled cynically at the memory. Even Dom's kiss had been an insult, harsh and punishing.

'So what makes you think this next meeting with him will be any different?'

'Because this business between our families means something to both of us,' she answered. 'We are both capable of putting our own animosity aside in an effort to find a solution.'

'Really?' His arched brow mocked her along with the tone he used. And Madeline sighed impatiently then began walking again on a sudden burst of restlessness, his perception of her just too uncomfortable to take standing still. It was a minute or two before Perry came up beside her again, and they didn't speak for a while, both seemingly lost in their own heavy thoughts as they walked on, the ice-cold water moving swiftly by beside them.

Then Perry muttered suddenly, 'I wish he'd walk by here right now. I would enjoy throwing the swine in the river.'

Madeline smiled, linking her arm through his and giving it a kind hug. 'You don't know how many times I've felt the same urge about Christina,' she confessed, remembering how, after Perry had finally broken off his engagement, Christina had enjoyed taunting him with a different man at every social gathering they attended. 'Only it was the nearest swimming-pool I used to want her to tumble into.'

His smile was rueful. 'Pair of idiots, aren't we?' he mused.

'Hmm,' Madeline agreed. 'Will you cover for me on Wednesday?'

Perry stopped walking so he could take her by the shoulders and turn her to stand in front of him. 'Will you promise to be very, very careful?' he demanded by return.

Madeline nodded. 'I promise to be the model of my mother's daughter,' she vowed gravely.

He laughed out loud at that, because Dee was such a coolly upright and serene member of Boston society. 'I suppose I can't get a better promise than that!' he conceded.

No, thought Madeline. She only hoped she had the power to live up to it.

'Having dinner with Perry, dear?' Louise repeated with the kind of smile growing in her eyes which made Madeline want to grind her teeth. 'That will be nice!

He's a nice young man. Your father likes him too. He has a way with him that makes him easy to be with.'

'I thought I'd use the London apartment to change,' she suggested.

'By all means do,' Louise approved, smiling slightly as Madeline's smooth change of subject told Louise that she was not going to get response to her subtle curiosity as to where Madeline's relationship with Perry was going. 'It may be sensible of you to stay over if it means a late night. Shall I let the Crowthers know you're coming?'

'Oh, would you?' She sounded suitably grateful. But really, she found it irritating the way Louise was so eager to help her so-called relationship with Perry.

Shades of the past, she noted heavily. It sent a cold little shiver chasing down her spine.

Nina was in a dreamy mood on Wednesday. And the ostensible reason for the shopping spree fizzled out into a schmaltzy trip down fantasy lane when Madeline couldn't seem to divert Nina from drooling over anything even vaguely babyish!

'Is there something you've not told us?' Madeline quizzed her stepsister when at last she'd talked her into stopping for coffee in one of the many small bistros scattered around London. 'Like—the premature pattering of tiny feet for instance?'

'Maddie!' Nina was shocked. She even went bright red with embarrassment. 'Charles hasn't—wouldn't—couldn't...'

'All right,' Madeline let her off the hook, 'I was only teasing. But brides don't usually spend a whole afternoon drooling over baby cribs and teddy bears.'

'Charles...' The Cupid's bow mouth quivered, and Madeline felt ashamed of herself. 'Charles wants our wedding-day to be absolutely perfect. He said he wants me to walk down the aisle in my gown of white with no hypocrisy to mar my day. My day, Maddie,' she sighed out dreamily, and went off into a world of her own while Madeline remembered another time and another place where a very different man had said those selfsame things to her. She, of course, being what she had been then, had scoffed at such silly, outmoded ideals. And now? she wondered thoughtfully. She would still scoff, she decided. When a man and a woman loved and desired each other, intended to bless that love with marriage vows, Madeline saw no reason to hold back on the rest just because of some old-fashioned custom which said the bride must be a virgin to wear white. Anyway, she'd intended to marry in pink—blush-pink—virgin or not. So what use would Dominic's grand gesture have been then? No one at the wedding would have thought him honourable to the last seeing his bride come to him dressed in pink! But then, she mused drily, by the time it actually came to ordering her wedding-gown, the two families would probably have manoeuvred her into changing her mind and wearing white instead. Just as they'd manoeuvred their whole relationship along the lines they'd wanted it to take.

And there, she recognised, was the real problem that had haunted her during her stormy relationship with Dominic. She had never been really sure whether he hadn't just been jostled along on everyone else's enthusiasm. The fact that he had always managed to draw back from making love to her had only added to her fear that maybe he was only marrying her because everyone else seemed to think it perfect—and because she seemed to amuse him. And even that had palled in the end. In the end, Dominic hadn't found her funny at all.

CHAPTER SIX

MADELINE appeared in the entrance to one of London's most exclusive dining clubs, too busy trying to hide the sudden bout of anxiety that had attacked her to notice the way every male present in the grand foyer turned to stare at her in open appreciation.

She was wearing a knee-length gown of aquamarine silk. Little more than a drape of fabric which crossed smoothly over her breast then fastened at her waist with two aquamarine-studded buttons, it really was a more daring dress than she would normally have worn. But she'd wanted to shock, show Dominic in some crazy twisted way just what he had turned down four years ago. Because she knew—without vanity—that the woman she had developed into by far outstripped the child with whom he had once considered himself to be in love.

Acquiring what her mother called mirror awareness had taught her to be self-aware—and how therefore to make the best of what she had.

So the dress accentuated the long curving grace of her slender legs, moved with the sensual sway of her body, skimming her breasts in a deep cutting V which gave tantalising glimpses of her shadowed cleavage, and hugging her narrow waist before draping itself almost lovingly around her rounded hips and long silken thighs.

Her hair had been left loose for a change, brushed until the dark waves gleamed and crackled around her shoulders, then lifted away from her temples by two sparkling combs. Her make-up, severely plain as always, was just a simple touch of dusky grey-blue to her lids,

and a raspberry-coloured lipstick that made the on-
looker yearn to lick it off. Possessing eyelashes so long
dark and naturally curling made it difficult for others
to believe they were actually her own. So she rarely put
herself out to further accentuate them.

But they were real enough. As Dominic Stanton well
remembered as he stood, momentarily stunned into
stillness by the vision she presented, hovering by the entrance. And even as her gaze settled on him and he
watched those same lashes flutter downwards to hide
whatever thoughts were going through her mind, his
senses were being jolted by the exquisite memory of what
those long lashes had felt like brushing against his skin
when he kissed her.

Madeline took in a controlled breath of air and smiled
a cool greeting as he approached. Her heart was
bumping, her hands trembling a little, but she hid her
nervousness by turning to hand over her jacket to the
hovering *maître d'*, the smile she sent him blinding out
any hint of tension in her.

'Still slaying them with your smile, I see,' Dominic
drawled as he came up beside her, his mocking gaze following the *maître d'* as he hurried away, flushing.

Madeline turned slowly back to face him, her own expression under tight control.

He looked fantastic. His dinner suit was conventional
black, his shirt just plain white, bow-tie slim and black.
Nothing extravagant about him, yet through it all he
exuded the natural magnetism which made him Dominic
Stanton, the compelling person he was, the dynamic
businessman he was. A hard man to ignore at any time,
he hadn't changed in that direction in four years, she
decided. His hair was still as dark and sleek as it had
always been, and cut in that neat, short, conventional
style he had favoured then. His face was still handsome,

strong-boned, smooth-lined—but perhaps in a harder kind of way—his body still that perfect male frame of tightly packed muscle and long strong bones. He would be thirty-two years old now—going on thirty-three, and showed four years more cynicism in the curve of his slightly smiling mouth.

But other than that, he was still the only man she had ever met who could make her senses pulse in awareness.

'Madeline,' he murmured. 'You look beautiful.'

Simply said, and all the more disturbing for it.

'Thank you,' she replied in a quiet, flat little voice that gave nothing away of what she was experiencing inside. Meeting him under cover of darkness had disturbed her deeply. And at the bank she had been too concerned for Vicky's feelings to allow herself the indulgence of studying him in the better light. But seeing him here, with nothing else to do other than absorb every single detail of him, made her want to turn and run from the turmoil of response he was creating inside her.

He took her arm. And in sheer instinctive response to his touch, she started, pulling free of his grasp before she'd realised what she had done. Dominic frowned, his mouth hardening as he glanced sharply at her. Then, determinedly, he took hold of her arm again, watching narrowly as she had to quell the urge to pull away from him a second time.

'We did a lot of things to hurt each other four years ago, Madeline,' he said grimly. 'But I don't recall ever giving you cause to flinch at my touch.'

He didn't? But then, Dominic was misunderstanding the reason why she pulled away. Which perhaps was better for her.

'Then I apologise for the—unnecessary reaction,' she murmured, 'you'll have to put it down to nervous anticipation,' using the truth to cloak itself.

A dark brow lifted at that. 'Did I catch a hint of acid on that smooth tongue just then?' he drawled.

He really was the most beautiful man, she thought with a sudden sense of overwhelming loss. 'You could have done,' she acknowledged, holding his mocking gaze with one of her own, 'but I do hope not.'

Her drawl seemed to irritate him further because his fingers tightened on her arm as he turned her abruptly towards the wide curving staircase which led up to the club's exclusive dining-room. 'So calm,' he mocked as they climbed the stairs side by side. 'So exquisitely beautiful, so very sophisticated. You know,' he said quietly, 'I was prepared to find you changed. Four years is a long time after all. But I never once considered the possibility that you would give in to Dee's ambition to turn you into one of her kind.'

'So you don't approve,' she concluded, though the derision she'd picked up in his tone rankled. She had, after all, only acquired what he himself had accused her of lacking badly.

He shrugged. 'In some ways the transformation is both delightful and rather challenging, but...'

'Ah,' she smiled, 'there has to be a but, I suppose.'

'The hair, for instance,' he observed. 'I saw the other Madeline marching directly to the nearest stylist's and having the lot shorn off as a defiant gesture aimed directly at me.'

'Ceremonially, of course,' she assumed, understanding him exactly. Dominic and her hair had once enjoyed a private love affair all their own. He had loved to bury his face in its silken mass and she had loved to feel his fingers combing through it, reacting to his touch with a shivering pleasure that had used to stir her blood.

His hand moved to her waist in an attentive gesture meant to guide her through the pair of open doors into the dining-room. And, unintentionally maybe, his fingers touched the silken edges of her hair. That instant tingling response on her scalp forced her to smother a gasp.

'I'm sorry to disillusion you, Dominic,' she murmured coolly in an effort to cover up her reaction, 'but I really wasn't that stricken.'

His step faltered. And Madeline gained the small satisfaction of knowing her reply had thrown him.

'You were,' he muttered. Then, before she could form any kind of protest, he added, 'We both were.'

She was saved from having to defend herself against that potentially provoking remark by the waiter, who was eager to see them both comfortably settled at their corner table. Dominic took her by surprise by refusing to take the seat opposite her and instead slipping into the one to her right.

'I hate talking across two dinner plates,' he explained the move as the waiter quickly rearranged the dinner placings, then disappeared, leaving the menus behind. 'If I am wining and dining a beautiful woman, then I want to enjoy her, not to peer at her over the top of some stupid table decoration.'

'This woman has not come here simply so that you can enjoy looking at her,' she said, dampeningly. 'You wished to talk. About Vicky, I believe you said.'

'Not yet,' he refused. 'First I want to know about you. What you've been doing with yourself, how you are— how you really are, Madeline.'

'I'm fine,' she said, then gave him a brief résumé of her life in Boston. 'It feels strange being back in England, but I expected it,' she concluded. 'Boston is my home now and I feel more comfortable there——'

His hand coming to cover one of her own where it lay on the table brought her to a breathless halt. 'Stop it, Maddie,' he commanded grimly. 'Stop trying to show me how wonderfully cool and sophisticated you've become, and cut out all that blasé spiel you've managed to fool everyone else with.'

'I don't know what you're talking about,' she denied, trying to remove her hand from beneath his, but he wouldn't let her, so she stopped the undignified struggle, gathered together all that impressive sang-froid he was being so scornful of and turned blandly patient eyes on him instead. His face was very close to hers. She could see the silver flecks lightening his slate-grey eyes, and remembered on a wave of sad nostalgia how once she had used to provoke the whole iris to turn black with passion. Angry passion, sexual passion; she'd never used to mind so long as she got a passionate response from him.

The silence between them grew, and slowly Madeline ceased to breathe as tension began to inch itself along her spine, watching his gaze flicker over her face, re-learning, taking in the changes and reacquainting himself with those things about her that would never change: the classical structure of her bones, for instance, and the creamy smoothness of her skin; the sensual fullness of her mouth, slightly parted now as she tried to breathe evenly; the small straight line of her nose, and those once so expressive eyes which now hid everything.

Slowly, as the silence stretched, and the tension altered to a fine buzz of awareness, the rest of the room began to lose itself in a blurred haze on the periphery of their tunnel vision, no mockery evident in either of them because for some reason they had both discarded it in this long private communion.

This, Madeline recalled achingly, was the Dominic she'd only ever seen when they were alone with each other—which had been so rarely. This was the one who could probe through the bright glittering girl she had been and home right in on the sensitive and vulnerable creature who hid within.

His hand was warm on hers. They were sitting close enough for their thighs to touch. She could feel the power in those corded muscles cloaked in expensive cloth, feel the ever-present animal magnetism of him. And old, forgotten sensations began to tingle just beneath the surface of her skin.

We once spent hours just gazing at each other like this, she remembered sadly. Her hand resting in his, the only real contact other than their eyes, the link to something so deep and meaningful that suddenly she wanted to cry for the loss of it.

'Boston was good for me,' she heard herself say, then blinked to break the disturbing eye contact. Dangerous, this, she warned herself with an inner shiver. Dangerous. 'I grew up there, Dominic. Don't try looking for that other foolish creature you once knew; she no longer exists.'

Something dark passed over his face—a hint of a sadness one felt with the fleeting memory of a loved one long gone from this life. 'And are you content with this new—image you project?' His voice was oddly gentle, and his eyes showed an alarming understanding.

Madeline removed her hand from his, and so withdrew spiritually away from him. Content? 'Yes,' she said. 'I'm content.' Happy? No. Alive? No. She took in a deep breath. 'And you?' she threw the conversational ball back at him. 'Are you—satisfied with your life? Vicky tells me you've outstroked your father in the money-making race. Success must taste sweet at that level.'

His mouth went awry in recognition of what she was doing. And at last he relaxed back into his seat as his own urbane mask slid smoothly into place. 'We all have our—successes to savour and our...failures to rue.' He looked directly at her, and Madeline knew that she had been one of his failures.

As if by tacit agreement, they both picked up their menus. Rocky ground was always best avoided whenever possible, Madeline mused ruefully. Their conversation had been drawing perilously close to rocky ground. And with an atmosphere tempered better to suit the occasion, they ordered and ate, using trivia to carry them through the interminable meal, and no one looking at them would ever guess that once they had been so closely in tune that it was sometimes impossible to distinguish where one spirit ended and the other began.

'I'm worried about Vicky,' Dominic said when at last they reached the coffee stage. A frown pulled his brows together.

'Yes, I am too,' Madeline agreed. 'Something has to be done about the situation, Dom,' she said grimly, too intent to notice the way she had shortened his name the way she'd used to do. 'It appalled me to come home and discover there was a feud in progress between our two families.' She turned an apologetic look on him. 'No one so much as mentioned it in their letters to me. And, quite frankly, I was annoyed to learn that the situation has been allowed to develop just because of our—our...'

'Stupidity,' he supplied for her. Madeline grimaced her dissatisfaction with the word but offered no other. She hadn't got one. And in any case, if she had, it would only have led to a discussion on their 'stupidity' which she had no wish for.

'Poor Vicky is caught right in the middle. And I'm afraid I can see no solution to the problem. She knows without my having to say it that she's more than welcome in my home, that Nina wants her to be bridesmaid at her wedding. Just as we understand that she can't do that without feeling she's letting her own family down.'

Madeline gave an impotent shrug. 'I wish...' She sighed, forgetting for the moment to keep her guards in place. 'I wish...'

'What do you wish for, Madeline?' Dominic prompted gently, his gaze fixed on her wistful face. She didn't answer him, lost in those same wishes in a way the old Madeline used to do. 'Do you wish the last four years had never happened?' he suggested, his hand going up to touch her hair as though it couldn't help itself, eyes suddenly dark on her. 'That we could turn back the clock to a time when we were all happy, and everyone loved everyone else with no dissension anywhere in sight?'

But there had been dissension, she remembered with a hardening of her heart. 'It's easy to look back and remember only the good times,' she declared. 'But only dreamers and fools do that.' She reached out for her coffee-cup and in doing so dislodged his hand from her hair. 'No,' she said firmly. 'I don't wish the last four years away. I only wish I could end this silly feud.'

'There is a way,' Dominic said quietly.

Slowly, Madeline replaced her coffee-cup. That tone was shiveringly familiar to her. Her father had used to use it when he was about to suggest something unpleasant. Dominic had too under similar circumstances. It usually accompanied the turning of their quick-calculating brains—and augured ill for all those involved.

'Whatever you're about to say,' she drawled, 'I'm sure I'm not going to like it.'

His smile acknowledged the point. 'I think I can positively say that you're going to hate it,' he drily agreed, then took her entirely by surprise by standing up. 'Come on,' he said, taking hold of her hand. 'Let's get out of here.'

It was automatic that she stood up too. 'But—where are we going?' she demanded as he began drawing her towards the exit.

'To my apartment,' he announced, tightening his grip when she instantly pulled against it.

'I'm going nowhere near your apartment with you!' she protested.

'Why? Too many fond memories there for you to stomach?' he mocked.

'Because I have my reputation to consider,' she informed him coldly.

'You never worried about silly things like that before.'

'I was a besotted child then.' They'd reached the curve on the upper landing where it joined the stairs before Madeline managed to pull him to a stop, tugging him around to see her anger. 'I am not going to your apartment with you,' she insisted on a driven whisper.

He stared at her flashing eyes for a moment, then simply turned without a word and began tugging her down the stairs.

'Dominic——!' Angry frustration almost made her stamp her foot, but then she remembered where she was, and with a tight firming of her mouth she slipped back into her cool shell. 'I refuse to let you cause a scene,' she informed him stonily, and let him lead her towards the exit.

'I was relying on that,' he said, glinting a mocking look at her flushed cheeks and gleaming eyes. 'Although,' he added ruefully as they reached the door where the *maître d'* was already waiting, Madeline's jacket at the ready, 'you worried me for a moment there.' Dominic took the jacket and slipped it around her shoulders. 'I really thought the old Madeline was going to jump out from behind the cool façade of hers, and land me a slap on the face!'

Her cheeks heated at memories of an incident when she had done just that to him and slapped his arrogant cheek. He'd been teasing her mercilessly all evening about a lovely blonde creature he'd spied across the room, mocking, taunting, downright provoking about how he'd like to put his shoes under her bed, or some such equally inflammatory remark. Until, in the end, the lid had come off her temper, and she had taken a swing at him, catching him unawares so that the flat of her hand made stinging contact with the side of his face. He had gone very still. The room had gone silent, every face turned in their direction as they recognised another Madeline Gilburn scene on the way. Then, quite calmly, quite dispassionately he had slapped her back.

The shocked gasps had rustled around the room. Dominic had stood very casually in front of her, waiting for her next response, all hint of teasing gone from his face. The silence had begun to throb all around them, and you could have heard a pin drop as Madeline stood trembling, her wounded eyes slowly filling with tears. Her mouth had begun to quiver, her hand going up to cover the mark on her cheek where his fingers had stung her. And, without a single word, she had just turned away from him and walked out of the room, leaving him standing there.

He had caught her at the door, his fingers curling around her wrist and tugging her roughly around to face him. He had glowered at her reddened cheek, at the tears streaming unchecked down it, and on a husky groan had pulled her into his arms.

'Forgive me,' he'd said. That was all, but he had said it with such a wealth of urgent emotion that it had shaken her.

'I'll come,' she told him quietly now.

Dominic frowned, surprised by her sudden climb-down. But then, she thought as they moved outside, he hadn't been inside her head just then, remembering a moment when her love for him would have had her following him to the ends of the earth without question.

The Stanton town apartment was situated on the very top floor of the bank itself. It was a rather unattainable place, huge, big enough to accommodate a whole convention of Stantons if the need arose. But because of the necessary tight security around the bank itself the family rarely used it, preferring to stay at one of the good hotels if a stop-over was required.

Except for Dominic. He, being the penny-pinching banker he was, saw no sense in paying out for hotel rooms when they had a perfectly good apartment going to waste right here.

He drove them up to the rear gates and allowed the night guard to check them out before he could open the huge gates which led to the private car park.

'Fort Knox,' he murmured as they climbed out of the car and had to wait yet again for security to operate the locking system securing the rear doors. 'Cold?' he asked when she shivered. He touched his fingertips to her cheek, eyes almost black in the half-light of the security light.

Startled by the unexpected caress, she glanced up at him, their gazes locked once again, and fine threads of electric tension began swirling around them.

'Madeline,' he murmured huskily, 'I...'

The doors swung inwards, bright fluorescent lighting flooding over them, cutting off whatever he had been about to say, and she experienced a profound sense of relief when he let it go, and instead guided her into the building, and straight into the waiting lift.

It took them swiftly upwards, ejecting them directly into the main foyer of the palatial apartment. Softly glowing table lamps greeted them, electronically switched on by the movement of the lift itself. Madeline allowed Dominic to guide her down the wide hallway to a door to the left which housed a room disturbingly familiar to her.

It was Dominic's own private sitting-room—more a den than anything else. It contained nothing fancy, only the creature comforts a man liked to have around him when he relaxed. And Dominic often relaxed here when pressure of work meant it wasn't worth him making the trip back to Lambourn in the evening. There was a desk, of course, untidily scattered with papers, two huge and chunky red velvet sofas, a comprehensively stocked drinks bar, a television set and expensive hi-fi stack, and the ever-present computer link with the bank.

Other than that, it contained all Dominic's personal bits and pieces, like the books on the shelves and the magazines scattered about. It wasn't a tidy room, but then Dominic never let anyone in here to 'mess' with it, and she had always liked coming here with him—mainly because it was one of the only places they had ever managed to be alone in comfort.

'That wasn't here the last time I came,' she observed, covering her nervousness at being here again by re-marking on a gold-framed painting she'd spied hanging on the wall opposite.

Dominic sent her a hooded look as he walked over to the drinks bar. 'No,' he murmured. 'It's a recent addition.'

Madeline walked over to take a closer look at it. It reminded her or something . . .

Unaware of Dominic's stillness as he watched her, she ran her eyes over the rather grand-looking black and white manor house standing within its own beautifully laid out grounds. Its grey-slated roof was shining as if a recent shower of rain had just washed it clean, the tiny diamond-leaded windows glinting in the new sunlight.

It reminded her of the old Courtney place that stood about halfway between her own home and the Stantons'. But where the years had been very kind and loving to the house in the painting, the Courtney place had been allowed to deteriorate badly over the years, its beauty lost.

A small sigh whispered from her lips. She had always shared a sad kind of sympathy with Courtney Manor. And seeing this lovely house looking as Courtney Manor should look brought those feelings back to her now.

'Who does it belong to?'

'What, the house or the painting?' Dominic quizzed, coming over to stand beside her and handing her a glass. 'The painting is mine,' he said. 'I just happened to come across it one day covered in the filth of centuries and looking nothing like it does now...it was the frame which initially caught my attention.'

'A junk shop?' Madeline could remember how Dominic couldn't resist rummaging around old junk shops. He had a passion for the old and unusual—not necessarily the valuable either, but things, objects which captured his interest—an addiction inherited from his mother, the family liked to tease. The Stanton house was filled with old curiosities, not all of them collected by his mother.

'You could say that,' he smiled rather cryptically. 'Once I got a closer look at the canvas, I decided it might be worth renovating—and as you see...' he indicated with his glass to the picture '...it was.'

'Can I buy it from you?' she asked impulsively, turning hopeful eyes on him. 'I'll pay you the full market price for it,' she added quickly when she saw the way he suddenly closed her out.

'Why do you want it?' He wasn't looking at her, but at the painting. But Madeline detected a tension in him that hadn't been there a few minutes ago.

'It—it reminds me of the Courtney place,' she admitted, shrugging because she was uncomfortably aware that she was revealing more than she liked of her inner feelings. Dominic knew all about her attraction to the Courtney place.

He said nothing though, narrowing his eyes on the picture as if trying to catch the resemblance himself. And they both stood in silent contemplation for a while.

'How serious is it between you and Linburgh?' he asked suddenly, and she jerked her head around to stare at him in surprise.

'What has that got to do with the painting?' she wanted to know.

He didn't reply, his gaze still fixed on the painting, a brooding quality about his stillness. Madeline frowned at him, wondering what was going on in that complicated mind of his.

After another long pause, he turned to look at her, his grey eyes dark and intent. 'You can have what's in the frame the day you can come and tell me that you've given Linburgh up for good.'

Her eyes widened in bewilderment. 'Why should you want me to do that?' she asked.

His crooked smile gave her her answer, and Madeline dropped her gaze from his, a sudden ball tightening the muscles in her stomach. Dominic still wanted her. He had just told her so.

CHAPTER SEVEN

SHAKEN, Madeline moved away from Dominic, going to sit down on one of the chunky sofas, struggling to hide what that revelation did to her.

It had taken four years to get over her last encounter with this man, and in just three short meetings she was sweeping those four years away as if they had never been!

She took a sip at her drink, eyes lowered because she was aware that he was watching her, waiting for her to say something, acknowledge what he had just so casually announced.

Over in one corner, the soft steady tick of one of Dominic's junk shop buys began winding up to chime the quarter. And automatically, Madeline checked the time on her own slender gold wrist watch. Ten-thirty, she saw just as the warm resonant sound of a Westminster chime began filling the room.

She glanced up at him, and their eyes caught and held, an old remembered heat washing right through her. He had undone his bow-tie, and it was hanging loose at his throat. The top few buttons of his shirt were open, too, allowing her a glimpse of his strong tanned throat. Her mouth went dry, and she swallowed some more of her drink, but the light white wine only agitated the commotion already going on inside her.

She took in a controlled breath, feeling her heart pumping heavily against her ribs. 'My relationship with Perry is none of your business,' she managed to say eventually.

'Perhaps not,' he conceded. 'But I would be obliged if you would tell me anyway.'

She should never have sat down. At least when she was on her feet she felt almost on a level with him, but down here, with him standing over her like that, she felt—diminished, under threat almost.

'We're still exploring the possibilities,' she told him, and left him to make of that what he liked.

'And Christina van Neilson?' he put in smoothly, bringing her fine brows arching upwards as she glanced at him.

'Been playing the sleuth, Dom?' she drawled, feeling the commotion going on in her stomach increase with the implications that idea offered.

His rueful smile committed him. 'The Linburgh-van Neilson affair was pretty well publicised, even over here. And the way I read it, Linburgh was not the one to call it off.'

Did he expect her to remark on Perry's broken engagement? 'As I said, we're still exploring the possibilities.' She refused to improve on her original answer.

Dominic gave an impatient sigh and at last moved from his stance by the painting. 'All I am trying to ascertain, Madeline, is whether or not he has a right to feel possessive of you.'

'No one has the right to feel like that about me,' she made quite clear.

He studied her for a moment, taking in the cool blueness of her stare, before saying quietly, 'I said earlier that I knew of a way to end this feud between our families.' And he smoothly shifted the conversation to the reason why they were supposed to be here at all. 'The way I see it,' he went on, 'is that since it all began because of you and I, then really it is up to us to make things right again.'

'Yes?' she said warily, prompting him to go on.

'By trying—as best we can—to put the clocks back four years.'

Madeline felt her composure slip, but she hid it quickly. 'Now, how am I supposed to respond to that, I wonder?' she questioned wryly. 'You know, I think I had better let you continue before making any response.'

Her mockery made his mouth twitch in appreciation. 'I thought,' he took up her challenge, using the lightness of his tone to keep her guessing as to his seriousness, 'I thought, that a—public reconciliation maybe—at the Prestons' this weekend, would——'

Anger flared briefly, the sheer cruelty of the idea stabbing into a wound so deep that it was still raw. 'And how are we supposed to stage this—wonderful reconciliation?' Her voice was so dry that it was brittle. 'Am I supposed to—demean myself at your feet again, so that perhaps you could graciously give your forgiveness this time and—*voilà*! Everything will be just fine and dandy again!'

Dom had the gall to smile. 'I rather saw it as my turn to do the begging this time,' he suggested. 'After all, the lady I see here tonight would not, I think, demean herself to anyone.'

True, Madeline agreed, only slightly mollified by the fact that he had at least noticed that *this* Madeline would cut off her nose rather than make a public spectacle of herself.

'Then how do you see us performing this—reconciliation?' She was curious, genuinely curious to know what dastardly plan he had cooked up for her. She knew Dominic, and the way his conniving mind worked. He had never approached a problem in a nice straightforward manner in his life!

But apparently he was still pondering over the theme Madeline had just so sarcastically discarded. 'I could prostrate myself at *your* feet, I suppose,' he murmured thoughtfully. 'And allow you to do the gracious forgiving. But...' He let out a pensive little sigh. 'Like you, I can't see myself in the role of humble supplicant.'

Neither could Madeline. Dominic was too proud a man to grovel to anyone.

'So, I wondered how you would feel,' he went on slowly, gauging his words, it seemed, to a very wary Madeline, for maximum effect, 'about us playing a little game of—now how shall I put it?' he murmured thoughtfully, eyeing her assessingly. 'Dalliance seems to say it well enough, but it's such an old-fashioned word, and I think *flirtation* probably says it better,' he decided. 'Do you fancy having a light flirtation with me, Madeline?' he invited, daring her with the mocking glint in his eyes.

The dreadful cheek of him alone made her smile. 'Oh,' she pouted, an affectation she had learned from her Boston contemporaries but rarely used. It just seemed appropriate here in this very false discussion. 'Flirting sounds so dreadfully capricious, Dominic.' Her voice was loaded with *savoir-faire* as she made a lazy gesture with her hand. 'We could, of course, just shake hands and pretend to make friends?' she suggested. 'Much more civilised than a flirtation. Shall we pretend to be *just good friends*, Dominic?' she said, aping his own lightly mocking tone.

'You aren't taking me seriously,' he accused gravely.

'Why?' She opened her blue eyes wide to him. 'Are you trying to be serious?'

He was the first to snap. 'My God,' he breathed. 'You really have it all off pat, don't you?'

With a deep sense of triumph stinging the blood to life in her veins, Madeline maintained the satirical air. 'You *are* being serious!' she gasped, shocked, and Dominic muttered something nasty beneath his breath.

He took an angry gulp at his drink. 'They didn't exaggerate, did they, when they said you'd changed beyond all recognition?' His mouth gave a bitter twist of disgust. 'I had hoped they meant just on the outside, but it goes all the way through, doesn't it?'

'What does?' she willingly took the bait.

'The blasé sophistication!'

'Why, thank you!' she drawled Boston-style, seething inside. 'It's so good to know that four years of my life have not been wasted!'

'Stop it!' he snapped, spinning away from her to slam down his glass in an act of burgeoning frustration. His spine was taut, the muscles in his shoulders bunching as he struggled to contain his anger.

Madeline watched him for a while, feeling oddly like crying when really she should be pleased at managing to better him so easily.

A sigh whispered from her. 'I'm sorry,' she relinquished heavily. 'I would like us to be friends, Dominic. For Vicky's sake if not for our own. But I don't know whether a friendship between you and me would ever work.' Too much bitter-tasting water had swirled under the bridge to support a rocky boat of friendship. And anyway, she added grimly to herself, he could still affect her emotions too easily. It was dangerous to so much as contemplate letting Dominic in close again.

She'd been hurt enough the first time.

She thought he wasn't going to bother replying, then he took in a deep breath and let it out again slowly. 'No,' he sighed. 'I do tend to agree with you on that point.'

He turned to face her, and they found themselves staring sombrely at each other again, the vibrations between them an odd mixture of remembered pain and a beautiful loving.

'Why did you do it, Madeline?' he said suddenly, his voice pitched low and thick. 'Why did you run away like that?'

She dropped her gaze. 'Let's not go back over old ground,' she advised heavily. 'I was very young and foolish, and you were...'

'What was I?' he muttered when she hesitated. Reaching for her, he grasped her by the shoulders and drew her to her feet. His expression was harsh, the dark glitter in his eyes burning wretchedly into hers. 'What was my excuse for what happened four years ago?' he demanded, giving her a small shake as if he couldn't help himself, his fingers clenching into the tender pads of her shoulders. 'It's all so easy for you to use your youth and impulsiveness as your excuse for your behaviour. But what excuse did I have? Tell me,' he growled, 'if you know, because it would certainly help me to understand something I've never been able to justify in four long miserable years!'

Tears sprang to her eyes. 'I don't know,' she whispered, shaken by the depths of his self-contempt. 'I just don't know what you thought or felt then, Dominic! How could I, when you never allowed me to know?' Her mouth turned down on a bitterness and frustration she had allowed to fester for four long years.

Clenching her teeth, she forced herself to calm down, sending him a smile that was every bit as blasé as he'd just accused her of being. 'Why not count your blessings and just be thankful for the lucky escape you had,' she drily suggested, 'instead of trying to understand what was, when all's said and done, a disaster?'

Instead of becoming angrier as she expected him to, Dominic surprised her with a rueful smile, his fingers slackening on her so that she was able to move away from him a little. 'Disaster covers it quite nicely, doesn't it?' he said. 'But,' he continued more seriously, 'as with all disasters, it's the confusion it leaves in its wake which causes the real problems.' He leaned back against the drinks bar, his hands sliding into the pocket of his black silk trousers, his expression grave. 'The confusion we left behind us, Madeline, has affected and still is affecting everyone attached to us. We have a responsibility to them to do something about it,' he concluded firmly.

'I'll get Nina to write out invitations to all the Stantons, inviting them to her wedding,' she suggested, 'and personally deliver them myself—I have no intention of joining this feud, Dominic,' she warned him. 'And both your family and my own will know that the first time I get the chance to show it—if, that is,' she then added ruefully, 'your family ever place themselves in my company again.'

'They stayed away from the Lassiters' to give you time to readjust, Madeline. It was not a personal message to you.'

'I know,' she said. 'I had managed to work that out for myself.' She lifted cool eyes to him. 'It isn't me who has gotten into the habit of reading an insult into everything, Dominic,' she pointed out. 'I can still remember how warm and caring your parents were to me.'

'They love you,' he said softly.

Her heart gave a painful squeeze. 'Yes,' she nodded. 'And I love them. And tomorrow evening I shall pay them a visit to tell them so—with Nina's invitations to sweeten the pill of having Madeline Gilburn threaten their peaceful lives again,' she added drily.

Dominic just smiled. 'And what do you think your father will have to say about that?'

Madeline made an impatient gesture with her hand. 'He shall just have to accept it,' she said stubbornly, then turned her impatient glance on him. 'I can't understand why you've let this go on for so long, Dominic! If I'd been at home, I would have made sure this silliness stopped long ago!'

'Would you?' he clipped. 'Then it just goes to show how little you know about the problem.' He eyed her thoughtfully from his casual stance. 'Did you know, for instance, that your father and mine almost came to blows over our break-up? That your father went as far as withdrawing all his accounts from our bank at a very awkward period for us—and he knew it? Did you also know,' he went on ruthlessly, 'that at this very moment your father is trying to get one of the big banks to back his latest brainwave but, as usual, everyone is wary of touching a Gilburn idea?' She was looking so bewildered that Dominic knew he was telling her fresh news. 'I'd finance him, Madeline,' he told her huskily. 'At the drop of a hat, I'd put the money up he needs to get his idea off the ground. But he's so damned pigheaded, he won't even discuss it with me!'

'Have you tried to approach him?' She was visibly shaken, her face gone pale beneath its smooth covering of make-up.

'Twice,' he nodded, turning grimly away to retrieve his glass. 'He didn't even bother to acknowledge my calls,' he informed her bitterly.

'The stubborn old so-and-so,' she muttered. Dominic was right. Her father was pigheaded! 'So, what do you suggest we do?' she asked, accepting at last that they were not going to solve anything the easy way.

He turned back to face her. 'We have to give an impression that you and I are considering making a go of it again,' he told her. 'It's the only thing I can think of which will melt the ice around them. They always did love the idea of you and me being a pair. Hell!' he rasped. 'I would even go as far as saying they took rather a large role in pushing you towards me! We all rushed at you when I come to think of it,' he added grimly. 'We were all guilty of hunting and cornering the spirited prey, forgetting that she had a habit of coming back spitting.'

'I seem to remember thinking you were the one cornered,' she murmured, remembering that awful night she had tried to seduce him.

'I was old enough to know my own mind.' Dominic dismissed. 'You weren't.'

'I don't flirt, Dom,' she made coolly clear, telling him two things in that brief statement: Firstly that she was at last beginning to take his suggestion seriously, and secondly that she had no wish to rake over the past. It resurrected too many bad memories.

'No, I do remember that,' he said soberly, eyes momentarily turned inwards on some private memory. He flicked a measuring glance at her, then grinned, the mockery back in his expression. 'How about a romance, then?' he offered.

'What . . . ?' Madeline drawled, matching his tone. 'Another one?'

'Oh, but this time it will be different,' he assured her. 'I mean, neither of us is in danger of making the same mistakes a second time, are we? You told me yourself on the phone only the other day that you learned your lessons thoroughly the first time around, and I . . .' His smile was something only he understood. 'The circumstances will be different for me. So what's to stop us indulging in a bit of romance? We surely are not immune to each other, so there should be no difficulty making it believable.'

A challenge? she wondered, and felt her nerve-ends tingle in temptation. The old Madeline had always possessed a weakness for challenges.

'And just think how it would throw all those vicious gossips into a flat spin seeing you and me together again.'

'All those poor matchmaking mamas,' she derided, 'groaning in despair.' Nina had told her about the way Dominic was haunted by ambitious mothers pushing their pretty daughters at him.

'Vicky as pleased as punch,' he went on after sending her a withering look for that remark. He always had hated his 'eligible bachelor' status. 'The parents would be so afraid that we might fall out again before they could get us married off that they would be around at each other's houses planning the wedding before either of us could draw breath! It could be——'

'Quite frightening.' Madeline said dampeningly. 'The next thing you'll be suggesting is that we got engaged again!'

'Why not?' he said, and it was his turn to be withered with a look.

'And what do we do when all the fuss is over, and everybody is liking everybody else again? When Nina is safely married—in the presence of the whole Stanton clan,' she mocked, 'and Vicky no longer feels pulled in two directions. Which just leaves you and me, with a sham of a romance to wriggle ourselves out of.'

'Can't we cross that bridge when we come to it?' he dismissed carelessly. 'Unless of course,' he then added silkily, 'you're afraid you may fall in love with me all over again.'

Madeline bristled instantly, lifting her fine brows at him in haughty disdain. 'Do you want this—pretend romance to go ahead or not?' she demanded.

'Sorry,' he smiled, 'but I just couldn't resist the taunt— I expected you to throw it right back in my face, but you didn't, did you?' Her tight-lipped refusal to make any comment on that last gibe made him laugh softly. 'Do we have a pact to play the besotted lovers to make our families comfortable again, or not?'

Madeline eyed him levelly for a moment. He was playing with her like a big cat with a defenceless little mouse. But she wasn't defenceless. Never had been, and Dominic knew that. So, what was he actually trying to manoeuvre her into here? She knew he still wanted her; he had said as much when he'd offered her the painting. And she knew that if she had any sense at all she should be turning around and walking right out of here before she found herself flailing in some very dangerous water. The trouble was, though, she couldn't help but feel a tingling buzz of excitement for the game.

It could be worth the risks, just to see all those condescending masks slip.

She took a deep breath. 'How do you propose to get this—deception off the ground?' It was an agreement, and they both knew it. 'And don't suggest the party at the Prestons' again,' she warned, adding sourly, 'I'm not into public reconciliations any more...I was put off them after a bad experience once.'

'A low hit, Madeline,' he admonished, then stood up straight, flexing his broad shoulders in a way that made her suddenly aware of just how tense he had been. 'You're having lunch with Vicky tomorrow, aren't you?' he enquired, and at her nod went on, 'I'll gatecrash, if you don't mind. And we'll take things from there, I think.'

'Fine,' she agreed, and turned suddenly to walk towards the door.

'Where are you going?' he shot at her, genuine consternation in his voice.

'Home,' she informed him coolly. 'We've discussed all we intended to discuss, and now it's time for me to go.' In truth, she was more than ready to escape from his proximity.

Too much of Dominic Stanton is bad for your health! she warned herself drily.

'Still infuriating when you want to be, I see,' he muttered, reaching her in three long strides. 'I like it, by the way,' he added.

'Like what?' she asked blankly.

'The new you,' he explained. His gaze ran slowly over her, lighting warning signals as it went. 'A sophisticated witch,' he mused. 'The mind boggles at the concept.'

'Dominic...' she warned, not in the mood for his brand of back-handed compliments.

'I've just thought of something,' he said, setting her nerves really jumping as he moved closer to her so that she was trapped between him and the closed door behind her. 'We'd better get in some quick practice while we have the privacy to do it.'

'W-what are you talking about?' she demanded warily, watching that old roguish glint enter his lazy dark eyes.

'Touching,' he said with a casual shrug. 'Kissing, that kind of thing.'

Latching on stupidly late, Madeline tried to push by him, only to find herself folded tightly against him.

'Don't!' she cried, but he ignored her, the smile on his lips half playful, half passionate. And it was the passion that set her struggling to get away. He simply waited for her to stop, eyes mocking her puny strength.

'You have the most delicious figure it has ever been my pleasure to hold,' he told her softly. 'This dress should carry a danger warning with it, it's so damned provocative.' His hands did a sensual slide down the side of her body from soft breast to firm hips, and Madeline couldn't hold back a small gasp of pleasure at his touch. 'And that mouth,' he murmured, 'that gorgeous raspberry mouth...'

'No——!'

Too late. He lowered his head and caught her lips, and everything alive in her went haywire and she fought not to respond to him. Clouds gathered across her mind, then cleared once they'd taken her back four years to when this was all she lived for. His body felt the same as it had then, still hard, strong and sensually assertive. His mouth was the mouth which came to her in her dreams and wrung her senses out with a frustrated longing. He even smelt the same, his skin, warm and satiny to the touch, evoking a hunger in her that she'd known all along had never been quenched. And the hot, sweet, melting sensation trickled insidiously through her body so that she had to hold herself stiff and unbreathing to maintain her resistance.

Dominic lifted his head, his eyes black where the pupils had engulfed the silver-grey iris. A dark flush stained his lean cheeks, and his mouth was parted, the air softly rasping her face as he breathed unsteadily upon her.

'Take another deep breath, Madeline,' he softly advised, his mouth so close to her own that the words vibrated against her trembling lips. 'You're going to need it, because that wasn't good enough. Not by a long way.'

This time everything that had been missing from the first kiss was there in strength in the second. Heat—a heat that burned her lips apart. Hunger—which sent his tongue snaking into her mouth to tangle greedily with her own. And passion—passion so intense that it forced a groan from her as her body caught fire, the flames dancing in applause for something her senses had been starved of for years.

Dominic muttered something, impatient because she was still putting up a token resistance. His arms tightened around her, one forcing her into an arch so that she had to cling to him to maintain her balance, the other burying itself in her hair, tugging her head back so that she was completely vulnerable to his demanding kiss. And she felt the heated press of his own response begin to throb against her.

It was her downfall. On a final distraught groan, she melted, and gave him what he was demanding of her, the hot sensual response of her own desire.

The kiss changed then, drawing a hunger from both of them that had them straining against each other as wave after wave of hot drugging passion swept over them.

When at last he dragged his mouth from hers, Madeline was so disorientated that she swayed dizzily, her limbs weak and trembling, heart throbbing loudly against her panting breasts.

Appalled with herself, she pushed him away, anger—thankfully—coming to her aid alongside the self-disgust which helped feed her voice with contempt as she bit out huskily, 'That was a mistake. You shouldn't have done that.'

'Why not?' He sounded husky and warm, his hand stroking her hair as though he were soothing a frightened fawn instead of a sexually furious female.

'Because you've just spoiled all our plans,' she informed him coldly, by quick degrees grabbing back her composure. 'I'll look for another way to heal the family breach,' she told him. 'But it won't be with any help from you!'

'Because I kissed you?' He sounded horribly mocking. Madeline felt her cheeks grow so hot that they burned her with humiliation. 'I had to do something to get through that wall of ice you've surrounded yourself in. God knows,' he derided, 'we'd convince nobody of anything with you freezing me off every time I so much as look at you!'

The derision brought her head up, her mouth beginning to tingle when she found her eyes drawn to the throbbing fullness of his still savouring the recent kiss. 'Well, now you won't have to worry about my reaction,' she said, turning stiffly away from him and placing a trembling hand on the door-handle. 'I want nothing more to do with you, Dominic. Please let me leave,' she added when he stopped her opening the door with the simple pressure of his palm on the wood.

'Don't be stupid!' he rasped, getting serious at last. 'You can't seriously be running away because of a couple of inconsequential kisses!'

Inconsequential! If she didn't get out of here quickly, she would hit him for that! On a strength born of anger, she managed to tug the door open despite his pressing hand.

'Is it Linburgh?' He followed her into the hall, his hand coming out to grasp her arm and pulling her to a protesting halt. 'Because, if it is, why not just say so instead of pretending all this—virginal outrage over a damned kiss?'

Madeline spun around on him then, her eyes alight with anger. 'No,' she said tightly. 'It is not Perry, nor any other man, come to that!' His face was no longer passion-softened but hard and watchful. As she glared at him, she saw him frown and begin mentally backing off, recognising the signs that the old and unpredictable Madeline had broken through her sadly slipped composure. But she didn't care any more; she just wanted to get out of his flat, out of his life by the quickest means possible. 'If you want to know the full unvarnished truth of it,' she bit out stingingly, 'then I'll give it to you. I came back here because I hoped four years was long enough to make my point. But it seems it wasn't. So I'll state it clearly so there should be no mistake. I am not available, for a dalliance, a flirtation, or a romance feigned or otherwise with you. And not because my feelings are involved with another man! But because I just don't want you!'

'Finished?' he clipped out coldly.

Madeline nodded.

'Then I'll take you home.'

He drove her to the apartment in a stony silence which was reflected in the granite hardness of his features, and Madeline sat beside him in a state of panicked near hysteria, wishing she had never come back, wishing she had just stayed in Boston where nothing nor anybody had the power to hurt her like this man did.

He escorted her all the way to her door before he delivered his own bitter reply to what she'd thrown at him.

'You're a liar, Madeline,' he said. 'Whether you're lying to me or, worse, to yourself as well I don't know. But you are—a liar. You responded to me in the exact way I responded to you—with a fire and a hunger built up over four long bloody frustrating years! Think on that while you lie in your bed tonight in lonely splendour. And think on this too.' He pushed his face up close to hers, his anger so strong he pulsed with it. 'If this—thing between our two families isn't resolved soon, not only will Vicky be more hurt than she is already, but your father will find himself in dire financial difficulties! He needs my support, and the only way he will get it is by you co-operating with me!'

His mouth landed a final stinging kiss to hers, then he was striding angrily away while she watched him go without a single word, too shaken by the unpalatable truth in what he'd said.

Tears filled her aching eyes as she watched him step into the lift and stab the 'down' button, felt a desperate need to go after him and even took a jerky step forward with that intention, before forcing herself to remain exactly where she was, and watching the lift doors slide across his hard, angry face.

The old Madeline was the one who had gone chasing after her angry man. This one held on to her pride at all costs.

CHAPTER EIGHT

HE HADN'T come. Why she had expected him to turn up at all, Madeline didn't know. But the wayward hope had lingered with her all through their first course and was just beginning to shrivel as they waited for their second course to be served. She had only picked at her food, too tense to eat. And Vicky was too engrossed in an involved story about a potential client she was trying to capture to notice Madeline's complete lack of appetite.

'I tell you, Maddie,' Vicky was saying excitedly to her inattentive audience, 'if I could land this one, I'd make my father eat every single one of all those deriding remarks he's made about women in a man's world! And he's so delicious to look at. He...'

Madeline glanced despondently around the crowded restaurant, wondering what all these people busily enjoying their lunches had to talk about. She couldn't think of a single thing to say herself. She wasn't hungry. She wasn't up to conversing with anyone. And she was tired from lack of sleep, and fed up.

Last night had been a disaster, so much of a disaster that she had spent the rest of the night pacing her bedroom floor, berating herself for thinking she and Dominic could spend time together in constructive discussion when even a fool should have expected it to degenerate into a slanging match! And not just a slanging match, she reminded herself heavily; the seduction scene had been pretty despicable too.

She despised him for that, if only because it had shown her how little he'd really cared about mending the family

111

feud if he had been ready to risk it by grabbing her like
that. And the new Madeline told her to forget him and
look in another direction for a solution to the problem—
while the old Madeline wanted to weep, because last night
had proved to her that, far from getting over Dominic,
she was still as vulnerable to him as she had always been.

Vulnerable. Perry had warned her but she'd taken no
notice. Her own common sense had warned her but she'd
taken no notice of that either! 'He led you around by
the nose,' Perry had taunted, and last night she had come
perilously close to being led by it again.

God, she couldn't believe she was still that gullible,
that big a fool! Dominic Stanton was just not——

It was then that she saw him, framed against the oak
and warm brass fixtures forming the restaurant entrance—and her heart stopped dead, then began to bump
heavily against her ribcage.

He had come after all. Despite all the bitter words
she'd thrown at him, despite the contemptuous ones he
had thrown at her, he had come, and she had to press
her teeth into her lower lip to stop it quivering on a
sudden wave of wretched elation.

So much for your new Madeline contempt! she
mocked herself as she watched the slate-grey eyes search
the busy tables.

He saw them. Over the top of Vicky's bobbing head,
she watched him fix her with a steady look, and had to
squeeze her trembling hands together beneath the table
as he began threading his way towards them, looking
unspeakably good in a dark pin-striped suit and crisp
white shirt, his lean face full of grim purpose.

'...American through and through...' Vicky was
saying. 'You know what I mean. All hard muscle and
sexy politeness. Has a face like Superman and the body
to go with it.' She paused to allow herself a small quiver.

But Madeline didn't see it; she was too busy watching Dominic come towards them, unable to break that helpless eye contact they'd achieved from the moment he walked in here.

He came to a stop behind his sister's chair. 'Hello, Madeline,' he greeted quietly, his hands going lightly to Vicky's shoulders as the poor girl almost jumped out of her skin at the sound of his voice, her eager chatter abruptly stemmed.

Madeline dragged her eyes from him to look at Vicky. She looked like someone who had been turned to stone, horror etched into her paste-white face. She looked back at Dominic. He was banking on her not making a scene in front of Vicky, but his expression was guarded—just in case.

'Hello, Dominic,' she answered quietly.

'Do you mind if I join you?' He requested smoothly.

'Dom . . .' Vicky's plea was huskily offered. She hated scenes of any kind, always had done. Vicky might give the impression of being a very liberated and independent creature, but she was also acutely sensitive to atmosphere. She just looked at Madeline through huge hunted eyes.

'Move your bag off the seat next to you so your brother can sit down,' Madeline told her gently, bland-eyed and bland-faced despite the turmoil going on inside her.

A waiter appeared at Dominic's elbow the moment he sat down, enquiring if the gentleman would like to order. Dominic shook his head. 'I'll just have coffee with the ladies when it comes,' he dismissed, and the waiter melted away, looking relieved that his table reservations were not going to be put out by the late arrival.

'How are the wedding plans going?' He swung his attention back to Madeline.

'Very well,' she replied. 'There's still a whole month to go before the big day, but you know Louise,' she smiled, 'she's well ahead with her planning.'

'Charles Waverley is a good man,' he said, no mockery. In fact, the mockery had been plainly missing since he arrived. 'I hope Nina will be happy with him.'

'I'm sure she will be,' Madeline glanced at Vicky. The tension the poor thing was giving off was awful, and she sat with her head bowed to the empty space between her cutlery, hands lost and probably clenched beneath the table. Madeline's eyes filled with tender pity as she shifted them back to Dominic. He gave a slight shrug, his mouth twisting ruefully. 'Do you know Charles well?' she asked, keeping her voice smooth and casual.

'Fairly well.' She saw his arm move, and guessed he had taken hold of his sister's hands. The suspicion was confirmed when Vicky glanced up jerkily to catch her brother's encouraging smile. 'Vicky fancied herself in love with him for a while, didn't you?' he teased her gently.

'I did not!' she denied, the tease effectively bringing her to life. 'He isn't my type! He's too—too...' Her voice trailed off on a fresh wave of discomfort, her head beginning to dip all over again when Madeline suggested,

'Bland?' And was rewarded with one of Vicky's rueful grins. 'I know what you mean,' she went on drily. 'He's so—so...'

'Bland?' Vicky murmured, and they both fell into soft laughter.

'Are women always so bitchy when they discuss a man?' Dominic drawled.

'Be glad you came along when you did,' Madeline murmured provokingly. 'You were next.'

'Really, though,' Vicky inserted quickly, fearing a row brewing, 'Charles suits Nina perfectly. She needs a man who'll protect and cosset her.'

'And you don't?' her brother mocked. 'I thought all women liked to be cosseted.'

'God, no!' Vicky shuddered at the thought, her earlier mortification all but gone. 'My ideal man must be strong-willed and damned determined if he wants to take me on. I need challenge in a relationship. Not total dependency. He has to be——' Her eyes had been flicking restlessly around the restaurant when they skidded to a halt, bring her words to a sudden halt also. 'God,' she breathed, then reached urgently across the table to grab Madeline's hand. 'It's him!' she whispered excitedly. 'No——! Don't turn around! It's the one I was telling you about before Dom arrived—you know . . .' she whispered at Madeline's blank look. 'The one I—— God,' she choked, 'he's coming this way!'

Dominic glanced curiously in the direction his sister was staring, and while Madeline watched both faces opposite her, unaware of whom they were looking at, she saw Vicky's face colour up, and Dominic's harden. He flicked his gaze back to her, and she almost blanched at the look of cold accusation he lanced her with.

'I had no idea you were expecting anyone,' he bit out frostily.

'I'm not,' she denied, frowning.

'Madeline!' the call went up, and she went very still for the moment it took her to understand what had changed Dominic from the genial companion into a cold and angry man.

Several things happened at once then. The waiter arrived with their main course. Vicky's eyes widened then hooded when she realised that the newcomer was not coming over to speak to her, but because of Madeline.

And Perry arrived at her side, confusing the waiter who was trying to serve them by bending down to kiss her cheek.

'What are you doing here?' she greeted him in surprise, thinking, Perry—Superman? Had Vicky gone blind?

'Same as you, I should image,' he grinned. 'Having lunch with Forman.'

Forman, Madeline repeated ruefully to herself. Superman. So Forman was Vicky's bigshot American client.

She got up, turning to smile in welcome to the other man. 'Forman, how nice to see you again.'

'Hello, Madeline,' he smiled back, reaching out to take her hand, then laughed when the waiter almost lost his serving dish. 'I think we're causing something of a traffic jam,' he drily observed.

The waiter finished serving as best as he could then got quickly out of the way, so that Madeline could then complete the introductions. Dominic was already on his feet. But it was Vicky she made known to the two men first, smiling as she informed Perry who her friend was.

'This is the girl you've been dying to meet,' she told him. 'My friend Vicky—Victoria Stanton—Perry Linburgh, Vicky,' she explained.

'The same Vicky Madeline tied to a tree during a game of cowboys and Indians, then proceeded to forget all about?' he asked, his hazelnut eyes alight with amusement.

Vicky laughed, 'She told you about that?' Her hand was taken and shaken warmly, brown eyes dancing to Madeline then back to Perry again. 'Did she also tell you about the time she cut me adrift in a leaky old rowing boat on the river then just stood by to watch me sink?'

Perry looked suitably horrified, 'You mean that god-awful river she had me walk along last weekend? I bet you were glad to see the back of her when she left!'

'Oh, no,' Vicky's denial was movingly sincere. 'I missed her dreadfully.'

'We all did,' Dominic put in, causing a small silence that only Forman Goulding did not understand. Dominic turned a brief smile on Perry. 'We've met before, Linburgh,' he said with a cool nod of his arrogant black head.

'I remember,' Perry was equally cool.

'Forman . . .' Madeline quickly brought the other man into their group. 'Vicky I think you've already met,' she murmured drily, 'but her brother I don't think you know. Dominic,' she turned glacial eyes on Dominic Stanton, 'this is Forman Goulding. He runs the European end of Linburgh's.'

Introductions completed, Perry glanced at his watch. 'I'm glad I've caught you, Madeline,' he said quickly. 'I was going to ring you later to find out what time you want me for this Preston thing on Saturday.' Madeline saw Dominic stiffen up from the corner of her eye. 'Only I have a meeting arranged for Saturday afternoon, which may mean me cutting it a bit fine if this party is an early starter.'

'No problem,' Madeline assured, an idea hitting her suddenly as she looked from Vicky to Forman Goulding who were talking quietly to each other. 'It's a "come when you arrive" kind of thing, so don't worry about messing up someone's dinner settings. And,' she went on casually. 'If Forman would like to join us this weekend, I'm sure Vicky wouldn't mind making up a foursome for the evening.'

Dominic was furious; she could almost feel him seething beneath the cool surface he was projecting. But there was more to her plan than just a little bit of match-making, and she was not going to allow him to spoil it.

'You did that deliberately to annoy me!' Dominic accused the moment the other two men had left, arrangements firmly made. He seemed to have forgotten his sister's presence at the table. But Madeline hadn't.

'Come to dinner on Saturday,' she invited her friend, 'then we can all leave from the same house.'

'Oh, Madeline!' Vicky groaned, the old problems reasserting themselves to make Vicky feel cornered. 'You know I can't come to your house! I wasn't even going to the Preston party because . . .' Not bothering to finish, she chewed anxiously instead at her bottom lip.

'See what you've done?' Dominic muttered. 'Now what the hell is Vicky supposed to do? Casually inform our parents that she's dining at the Gilburns' on Saturday, and expect them to just accept that without feeling hurt?'

'You come too,' she said, knocking the wind right out of his sails, then made a sound of impatience. 'Think about it!' she sighed. 'It's the ideal solution! Your father can't afford to offend people of Perry's and Forman's standing! He must know that Vicky is chasing Forman's account. The fact that both men are spending the weekend at my home shouldn't prejudice Vicky's chances. Isn't it a man's motto not to allow the personal to intrude on business?' she challenged.

'Hey—you're right!' Vicky put in excitedly. 'Daddy can't possibly protest!'

'But Madeline's father can,' Dominic inserted dampeningly, 'and he has no qualms at all about mixing personal with business.' His slate gaze derided Madeline with a look before he turned back to his sister. 'Have you forgotten, sister, dear,' he drawled, 'that the Stantons are no more welcome in the Gilburn home than they are in ours?'

'So, what do you propose we do?' Madeline said. 'Keep avoiding each other like the plague just because of a silly rift that should not have been allowed to develop in the first place?'

'I told you my solution last night,' he snapped.

'Yes, and I told you what I thought of it!'

'Last night?' Vicky put in sharply. 'You two saw each other last night?'

'Swine,' Madeline muttered at Dominic, going red.

'Then this isn't the first time you've met since that time at the bank last week?'

'You asked for it,' Dom said, unrepentant.

'How many other times have you met?' Vicky demanded suspiciously.

'Once was enough!' Madeline said bitterly.

'Twice,' Dominic corrected silkily. 'Remember the time down by the river?'

'My God, you sneaky pair of devils!' Vicky gasped.

'This food is cold,' Madeline sighed, sitting back in her seat.

'Does anyone else know you've been meeting in secret?' Vicky was like a dog gnawing at a bone, asking questions, forming her own answers while the other two fought a battle of their own. 'What about Perry Linburgh?' she wanted to know. 'Or Diane Felton, come to that?'

Madeline's attention was suddenly caught, and she lanced Dominic with a look. 'And who,' she demanded silkily, 'is Diane Felton?'

'You'll be able to meet her on Saturday night.' Dominic smiled an acid smile. 'I shall personally introduce you both—when I bring her to dinner at your home!'

'Oh, you won't like her, Maddie,' Vicky put in absently, still trying to grappling with her new-found knowledge. 'She's one of those really sophisticated bitches he favours these days. She——'

'Watch it, half-pint,' her brother warned, then added deridingly to Madeline, 'You know the type, darling. Not very different from the new you.'

'I won't have it.' Edward Gilburn huffed. 'I won't have that Stanton man in my house!' Madeline sighed impatiently, and he glowered at her for it. 'And quite honestly, Madeline,' he went on haughtily, 'I am amazed at you for inviting him after what he did!' He shook his silvered head in disgust. 'I thought you'd learned your lesson about him the first time around.'

'Edward!' Louise snapped, and it was so unusual for her to shout at her husband that he almost sat down in surprise. 'Perhaps you should try considering Madeline's difficult position in all of this! She didn't ask you to fall out with the Stantons.'

'Us, Louise, us!' he corrected forcefully.

'You, Edward,' Louise insisted. 'It was you and James Stanton who had the fall-out; Beth Stanton and I just got carried along on the tide, while poor Vicky and Nina got trapped right in the middle! How do you think it feels to Madeline to know her childhood friend is not welcome in her own home?'

'Did I make a single protest about Vicky?' he countered. 'Vicky is welcome here any time she wishes!' he exclaimed. 'But her brother is another kettle of fish entirely. He hurt my baby, and...'

'They hurt each other, Edward. Please remember that. And Madeline is right. It's time it was all forgotten.'

Madeline was beginning to rue the moment she'd had her brainwave this lunchtime, when a soft, gentle voice from across the room piped in, 'I have an idea.' And all faces turned in surprise in Nina's direction, and she smiled uncertainly. 'The way I see it,' she said tentatively, 'is that Madeline has as much right as any of us to invite whom she pleases into her own home. But, on the other hand, I don't think she should expect Daddy to calmly sit down to dinner with a man he hasn't spoken to in four years——'

'Thank you, angel,' Edward Gilburn said stiffly, puffing up because Nina was giving him her support.

'So,' Nina took a deep breath. 'I think we should let Madeline have her dinner party—in private,' she suggested. 'And, so no offence is taken on the Stanton side, we'll let everyone believe that we have another engagement—to dine with Charles at his home. That way nobody is made uncomfortable, are they?'

Madeline dressed with a deliberate intention of making an impact in an exquisite gown of dark red velvet with off-the-shoulder little sleeves and a plunging neckline. The skirt was short and tight, with a simple slit at the back which gave glimpses of her silken thighs when she moved.

She swept her hair up high on her head and secured it with two gold combs. At her ears she wore large gold loops which swung as she moved and a thick gold chain circled the base of her slender throat.

Perry pronounced her ravishing when he saw her, but she felt herself fade away into nothing when Dominic walked in with Diane Felton on his arm. She wore white, a frosted, shimmering white that skimmed her svelte slim figure as she moved. Flaxen-haired and milky-skinned, she made Madeline feel dark and heavy by comparison.

'He certainly has taste, I'll give him that,' Perry murmured at her side, watching Madeline's too-revealing face as she studied the other woman. 'Would you like me to lure the Snow Queen away so you can move in?' he suggested tauntingly.

'Snow Queen just about says it,' she gritted bitchily through stiffly smiling lips as she watched, with unwanted resentment, Dominic lower his dark head to murmur something in her shell-like ear, leaving Perry laughing softly behind her as she walked forward to greet her guests, aiming her attention at Vicky first.

'You came.' She smiled warmly at her friend and kissed her on both cheeks. 'I did wonder if you would.'

'It was touch and go for a time,' Vicky admitted. 'I'm afraid I turned coward and left Dom to do the arguing with Daddy.'

'And why not?' Madeline sent the listening Dominic a mocking glance. 'He has to come in useful sometimes, I suppose. Hello, Dominic.' She held out a hand to him. 'How nice of you to come.'

His mouth twisted at the polite little greeting. 'I just couldn't resist,' he drawled, taking her hand and holding on to it when she would have pulled away from his burning touch. 'It's been such a long time...'

'Darling?' Diane Felton's voice was as light and as colourless as the rest of her. She turned superbly anxious eyes on her man. 'Are you two going to be rude to each other?' she enquired pensively.

She knew about their past relationship, Madeline made a dry note, then wondered acidly if there was anyone living in Lambourn who didn't know.

'We are never rude,' she assured the other woman, smiling her best social smile. 'You must be Diane.' She wriggled her hand out of Dominic's to offer it to the blonde, who took it with a perfectly cold smile.

'Diane, this is Madeline,' Dominic made the introductions. 'Just back from Boston and ready to take Lambourn by storm.'

'Already taken it,' Perry appeared beside her, his arm going comfortably around Madeline's waist. He turned a charmer's smile on Diane Felton. 'I've had to fight off more than one potential beau since we arrived,' he explained.

'You're my beau,' Madeline softly assured him. 'Perry Linburgh,' she informed Diane.

The wide-spaced eyes the colour of a summer storm suddenly came to life, and revealed a surprising intelligence. 'I've heard of you, Mr Linburgh,' she said. 'I sit surrounded by your name every single day!'

'You do?' Perry drawled. 'Tell me more!' And true to his word, Perry deftly drew the Snow Queen away.

'Diane is a computer expert,' Dominic explained. 'Her office is a minefield of electronic gadgetry, all with the Linburgh logo emblazoned on it.'

'She's—lovely,' Madeline said as she watched them go, relieved that the little truth hadn't stuck in her throat.

'Just my type,' Dominic agreed, then bent to murmur in her ear. 'She really is very nice, you know. You might even find yourself liking her if you give her a chance.'

'I never said I wouldn't,' she protested.

He was laughing at her. 'Your expression gave you away, green eyes.'

'I haven't got green eyes.' She frowned at him.

'No?' he mocked. 'They certainly looked green to me a moment ago. But then,' he added whimsically, 'perhaps it was a trick of the light.

'Don't play games with me, Dom,' she said impatiently, angry because he was right and she was seething with jealousy. 'I thought I made it clear to you the other night that I don't like it!'

Suddenly he was grim-faced. 'And I don't like the way Linburgh touches you all the time,' he threw back.

'If you two don't get your act together,' Vicky put in tightly, 'you'll be putting our families through another scandal—I can see it coming!' With that she stalked away to join Forman, who had taken on the task of mixing cocktails.

'She's of the unshakeable belief that you and I have been meeting secretly every day since you arrived back,' Dominic told Madeline, adding ruefully, 'I'm not sure if she's miffed because neither of us have confided in her, or worried for us both in case we make as big a mess of it this time around as we did the first.'

'But that's rubbish,' Madeline dismissed. 'Didn't you tell her so?'

His eyes mocked her naïveté. 'Do you honestly think she would believe a denial after the performance we put on the other day?'

'That was all your fault,' Madeline accused.

'Fifty-fifty,' he corrected admonishingly. 'We have to take the blame for our sins both past and present on a fifty-fifty share-out, Madeline.'

'And the future?' she asked. 'What will the share-out on that be?'

'Oh, that all depends on how you behave,' he murmured, unmoved by her sarcasm.

Madeline turned fully to face him, glorious, with her blue eyes sparking. 'I warned you, Dominic,' she said tightly. 'I won't play games!'

'Too late, darling.' He touched a finger to the tip of her small straight nose. 'The game began at the restaurant the other day. You could have put a stop to it then if you'd really wanted to.'

'God,' she choked, spinning away from his disturbing touch. 'You're insufferable!'

'I know,' he sighed just behind her. 'One of my worst failings, so I'm told.'

'Why are you doing this?' She was busily watching the brilliant way Perry was holding everyone's attention away from them, but her own attention was stingingly locked on the man standing directly behind her.

'Why? To set the record straight of course,' he drawled. 'Blame it on the accountant in me. I can't stand long-outstanding debts.'

'I owe you nothing!' she spat at him furiously. 'And just remember,' she warned, 'we're all here tonight for Vicky's sake. Not so you can——'

'Strange,' he cut in smoothly. 'I thought we were here so Madeline Gilburn could show us all how wonderfully grown-up and sensible she has become.'

She moved angrily away from him, his soft laughter gnawing at her nerves. For the rest of the evening she played the gracious hostess to the hilt, and no one, not even Dominic, could have faulted her performance.

CHAPTER NINE

'OK, I'M not too big to admit it. I'm impressed,' Dominic said, hours later, when Madeline had at last paused for breath and allowed herself to stand back and view her triumphs with a well deserved metaphorical pat on the back.

Only one potentially explosive incident had taken place since her altercation with Dominic before dinner, and ironically it had happened as they were preparing to leave her home, and Madeline realised she'd left her wrap in her room.

'I'll get it,' Perry offered, already striding for the stairs when he added questioningly, 'The black velvet thing I saw draped over your chair, is it?'

'Yes,' she called, smiling warmly after him before turning back to face the hallway to find Dominic's gaze narrowed on her. He stared coldly at her for a moment, then flicked his gaze up to where Perry was disappearing along the upper landing. Madeline felt the air lock tight in her throat, a dark blush running angrily up her cheeks when she realised what was going through his suspicious mind. Her chin came up, eyes defying him to question Perry's right to be familiar with her bedroom. He said nothing but his contempt was obvious.

Perry came back with her wrap, and lightly caressed her nape with his lips before settling it over her shoulders. Dominic spun his back to them and, sharp as always, Perry noticed the movement and sent Madeline a smugly amused look which told her he had done it all quite deliberately.

'You're a devil,' she murmured drily to him.

'He's seething,' he remarked unrepentantly.

'And I repeat, you're a devil.'

Perry just laughed and placed his arm warmly about her shoulders as they walked outside. Dominic watched them appear, then deliberately turned Diane to face him and kissed her on her mouth.

Madeline froze, taking his form of punishment like a punch in the solar plexus. Perry's arm tightened consolingly. 'Sorry,' he murmured. 'My fault.'

'Let's go,' was all she said, but inside she was a seething mass of the kind of emotions only the old Madeline had used to experience. And she was glad to climb into the back of Perry's bright red Lotus so that she could hide her face in the dim interior of the car while she brought herself firmly back under control.

They drove to the Prestons' in two cars, Dominic driving Diane while the rest of them travelled with Perry. By the time they all arrived at the Prestons' home, it was getting late. Dominic and Diane were already waiting for them at the door, Diane huddling into her warm fur jacket against the cold April night air.

'You should have gone in,' Perry quizzed their sense in waiting out in the cold.

'Solidarity is the order of the evening.' Dominic levelled his cool gaze on Madeline. 'Isn't that so, darling?' he drawled.

'Yes,' she said firmly, taking in a deep breath for courage.

'Have I missed something important to do with this evening?' Forman drawled sardonically.

'Not a single thing,' Vicky murmured very drily as all six of them walked into the Prestons' home.

For impact value, their arrival was perfect. No one, but no one, could misunderstand the statement being made when Madeline Gilburn and Dominic Stanton arrived so obviously together—but with different partners each. Forman glanced at the sea of astounded faces turned their way, then down at Vicky, who was trying hard to look nonchalant—but her fingernails were almost cutting into his flesh where they gripped the crook of his arm.

'I did miss something,' he murmured softly. 'I have to assume that all this tension is caused by two certain opposing factions in our group?' he suggested curiously.

'You mean you don't know?' Vicky looked up at him in surprise. 'I thought Perry would have explained it all to you.'

'Not a single thing,' he mocked her own dry answer of earlier.

'It's a long story,' she whispered as their host and hostess, looking a trifle harassed, approached. 'I'll explain it to you later.'

'You certainly stage-managed it all beautifully,' Dominic was saying ruefully to her now.

Her cheeks were glowing, eyes sparkling with the success of her efforts. Over to one side of the crowded room, her parents were talking to Dominic's parents. There was restraint there, but at least they had seen the folly of carrying on a feud their children had so obviously discarded.

Madeline had led her party around the room with the grace and charm of the true socialite, introducing, chatting, laughing lightly, always in control and knowing exactly what her next move would be.

With a diplomacy learned from the highly experienced Dee, she'd sent Perry off to dance with her mother, Dominic to dance with his, and Vicky had found herself inviting her own father on to the dance-floor while

Forman took care of Diane so that Madeline could grab her own father. As if it had been well rehearsed, they all came together at the end of the dance beside a wide-eyed Nina who had witnessed the whole thing from the sidelines, her fiancé standing sentry behind her.

'So I don't have to prostrate myself after all. Shame,' Dominic sighed. 'I was almost looking forward to it.'

'As you see,' Madeline turned her glowing face up to him, 'such dire actions are not necessary. And I did it without——'

'Without needing to mount even the lightest hint of romance with me,' he completed for her, sounding mockingly saddened about it. 'And,' he went on, 'without giving all these—lovely people the nice juicy scene they've been so looking forward to since Madeline Gilburn arrived back home.'

'Vicky's glowing,' she pointed out, forcing him to remember the main objective of the evening.

Dominic swung his glance over to where his sister was talking animatedly to Forman. 'The poor man,' he murmured. 'I wonder if she's drowning him in FT index points and the Japanese stockmarket.'

'Dominic!' Madeline rebuked. He just laughed; he had meant no malice towards his sister. 'Where's your Snow Queen?' she asked, wishing he would just go away. People were beginning to look.

'I've deserted her, for a black-hearted pagan,' he said. 'Where's your faithful beau?'

'Dancing with your Snow Queen,' she noticed then, the amused glint in Dominic's eyes telling her that he had seen them too.

'Come on.' He reached for her hand. 'Let's you and I do the same thing.'

'But I don't want to dance with you!' She tugged pro-
testingly as he began to draw her towards the dance-floor,
her heart already beginning to hammer at the prospect.

'Of course you do,' he insisted. 'You don't want to
spoil everything now, do you? They'll have noticed, you
know,' he added succinctly, 'that you've danced with
everyone else in our party except for me.'

Beaten, she went silently into his arms. Dominic drew
her close, the flat of his hand pressing against the base
of her spine. Their bodies fitted together as perfectly as
they had done four years ago, and he swung her away
to the haunting sound of a Gershwin melody.

'Do you know you are the most beautiful creature in
this room tonight?' he said suddenly, surprising her into
glancing up at him. He caught her gaze and held on to
it. 'Four years ago you were beautiful, excitingly so. But
now...' His silken sigh disturbed the thick fall of her
lashes, making them flutter. 'Perhaps you needed those
years with Dee to learn how to deal with it all...' he
added soberly. 'There's certainly more danger in the new
self-controlled Madeline than there was in the younger,
more easily read one.'

'Danger?' She picked up on the word because she
wasn't sure she liked it.

'Danger,' he repeated huskily, looking grim all of a
sudden. 'All beautiful women are dangerous, but you,
Madeline, have the power to be lethal.'

'Don't be silly,' she admonished, giving a soft dismissive laugh, her heart beginning to race. 'You make
me sound like some deadly weapon!'

'And there is the danger,' he said grimly. 'When you
decide to "go off", as they put it, it promises to be one
hell of a show. And I intend to be the only one around
to watch it happen.'

'Stop it, Dom,' she whispered, glancing anxiously around her in case people were watching them.

'What's the matter,' he taunted, 'afraid this may become an action replay of the last time we danced?'

She shuddered, the mere idea of it making her feel sick inside. 'I've told you, I don't make scenes any more.'

'Good,' he said, 'then just shut up and dance.' He pulled her closer to the warmth of his body, and they danced on in silence for a while, Madeline too aware of all the curious eyes on them to relax.

But eventually, as one tune drifted into another, and they lost their interest value when it became obvious that she and Dominic were not going to treat them all to a scene, she began to relax, let her body lean more reliantly on Dom's, and surrendered to the weak pleasure of being in his arms.

The continual brush of his thighs against her own and the slow caressing movement of his hand against her back eventually sent her eyelids flickering shut, soothing her into a state of near euphoric pleasure until the dance, the music, the people all began to fade into the background of her consciousness as the awareness always buzzing between them swamped out everything else until her head was full of it, her senses homed on to the alluring smell of him, the touch, the sweet sensual taste where her lips kept brushing against the silken warmth of his throat. She sighed softly, her breath moistening his flesh where it brushed, and Dominic touched his mouth to her cheek, his hands drawing her even closer. They danced on and on, the world around them melting further and further away as they moved.

The Prestons' home was old and rambling, old enough to possess its own ballroom built in a time when the rich had played more than they worked. And Dominic danced her around and around the floor until she felt dizzy, disorientated, too weak to even want to fight the feelings busily resurrecting themselves between them. This, she decided, was what she had been born for. And her four years away had done nothing—nothing to erase this need in her for this one man.

'This isn't what I want to be doing, Madeline.' His mouth was a trembling whisper against her ear. 'I want to be alone with you.'

'Please don't, Dom,' she pleaded, groaning at her own weakness as his words sent her swaying closer to him.

'Too late,' he murmured in husky triumph, and swung her away from him so suddenly that she stood blinking up at him, the amused gleam in his eyes only half concealing the passion burning beneath.

Madeline gazed bewilderedly around them, stunned to find the music gone, the hum of light chatter; and that Dominic was quietly closing the door of the Preston's beautiful book-lined study.

He had danced her out of the ballroom and across the hall into this room without her even being aware of it! Appalled that, while she had believed him as absorbed in their dance as she had been, he had actually been coolly planning to get her alone like this, she flung herself away from him, and stood trembling with angry humiliation.

'I am not going to fight you for supremacy over that door, Dominic,' she informed him coldly. 'I would prefer if if you would just move away and kindly let me pass.'

His eyes were lazy on her angry face, the proud lift of her chin, the faint quiver of her mouth which said she hadn't quite managed to grasp back her self-control. A fire burning in the Prestons' grate surrounded her in a warm rousing glow, highlighting the pagan blackness of her hair, the perfect symmetry of her slender figure, the agitated rise and fall of her breasts beneath the passionate red velvet. Her skin, pale and smooth, and her eyes, dark and luminous, like sapphires on fire themselves.

'You don't want to go anywhere, and you know it,' he said, suddenly no longer sleepily amused, but angry— angry enough to make her back warily as he began moving towards her. 'Like me, you want this so badly that you're actually trembling with it, so damned hungry it's eating you up inside!'

He reached her, and her heart leapt as his hands came firm and determined to her hips, pulling her against him. She put up her hands to his shoulders to hold him off, but they were shaking so badly that they held no strength. And his tight smile said he knew it.

'Four damned years trying to fight something that has no intention of going away!' he muttered. 'What a waste, Madeline. What a damned stupid waste!'

She made a small sound of denial, but it came out as nothing more than a strained little whimper, and on a husky growl that sent her senses leaping his mouth claimed hers with a burning demand and they were kissing with a frenzy which left neither of them with any barriers to hide behind.

The fire was hot on her back, the front of her burning from the heat of his body pressed hard against her, alive and throbbing with a need that sent a thick insidious heat drenching through her.

'Meet me later,' he pleaded huskily.

'Where?' It never occurred to her to refuse. The old excitement was running like fire through her veins, the old compunction to go where her instincts took her— where Dominic led. She felt suffused with the power of it, alight and alive.

'At the boathouse,' he said, reviving memories which had her groaning painfully, and, on a soft growl, his mouth came back to hers to deliver a kiss hard with angry frustration. 'As soon as you can get there.'

He put her away from him then, holding her with his arms locked so that she couldn't sway closer to him. And on a surge of that old Madeline desire to pierce his control, she ran the flat of her palms along his shirt-front where the skin burned beneath—then on down his groin, fingertips tantalising the taut sensitive muscles so that they contracted violently to her touch. Her eyes lifted, catching his with a look so utterly salacious that he had to shut his eyes to it.

'Witch,' he whispered tightly. 'Do you want me to take you here where anyone could walk in and catch us!'

Her hands jerked away from him; she was horrified because she was suddenly aware of how easily she had slipped back into the old Madeline ways, driving him further than any decent woman had the right to do. 'No,' she whispered, and wrapped her arms around herself as a shudder of self-contempt rocked through her.

As if he sensed what she was feeling, Dominic was suddenly behind her, his own arms coming to cover her own, hugging her back against him. 'I want you, Madeline Gilburn, ex-love of mine,' he murmured huskily against her hot silk cheek. 'Any way I can get you. I've never stopped wanting you. The new Madeline, the old Madeline—any Madeline I can have will do, so long as she is *my* Madeline!'

She quivered, too, too susceptible to the passionate possession in his words to refuse. 'You and I, this time,' he promised. 'You do know what I'm saying, don't you? I'm talking about us trying again. Being whatever we want to be to each other, no family intervention, no arm-twisting, no outside collusion—understand?' She nodded, and was rewarded with his mouth feathering heatedly across her cheek. 'You won't let me down?'

She shook her head. No, she thought bleakly, she wouldn't let him down. It was, after all, only what she wanted herself. Dominic was right, and the four-year-long separation had made not an ounce of difference to this—this madness which was their passion for each other.

'I'll be there,' she promised. And he let out a long breath, his body relaxing behind her.

It was gone three in the morning by the time Madeline led her saddled horse from the stall and took the frisky mare over to the hard-packed soil before mounting her and turning her in the direction of the river.

The rest of the house was asleep at last. The grey stone walls looking cold and bleak against the murky April darkness. They had not returned from the Prestons' until an hour ago, and, exhausted, everyone had drifted immediately to bed—except for Madeline.

She had paced her bedroom, trying to analyse her feelings for Dominic, worrying if she was doing the right thing meeting him, telling herself it was pure folly to make herself vulnerable to him again, and battling to subdue the delicious clamour of anticipation she had not allowed herself to feel in years.

They had stayed away from each other for the rest of the evening, she sticking closely to Perry and Dominic to the lovely Diane. But that didn't mean they weren't excruciatingly aware of each other every second. Wherever she looked she seemed to find the fierce glitter of his eyes on her, keeping her senses heightened, and reminding her of her promise.

The turf was hard beneath the horse's hoofs, pounding out an even beat as they galloped across the open countryside. A low ground mist enveloped everything in a soft skirt of billowing white. She was making for the river, and the closer she got the thicker the mist became, until by the time she entered the wood it swirled in and out of the tall trees, leaving its silvery cobweb patterns on the low growing shrubs. She let Minty pick her own way through the dry undergrowth, unable to see the way herself through the mist, taking it slowly, trusting the horse to take her where she wanted to go.

She saw Dominic's black mount as she came to the edge of the clearing and urged Minty carefully forwards. A hand came out from nowhere, grasping the reins and making Madeline gasp in fright. 'It's OK,' Dominic's deep quiet voice soothed her. 'Let me lead you,' he said from somewhere inside the swirling mist.

He tethered the horse next to his own, then reached up to help her dismount, his hands firm about her waist, pulling her against him before lowering her booted feet slowly to the ground.

'I wondered if you would come,' he murmured huskily. 'I worried that you might change your mind.'

'I said I would,' was all she said, and he nodded, accepting what added up to a small rebuke. For all her faults, Madeline had never gone back on her word once given.

Dominic stepped back from her, and the mist closed in between them. Startled by how quickly it had blotted him from her view, she put out a hand in search of him.

'Not the ideal morning for this.' She heard him laugh softly. 'Still...' Her hand was taken and she felt herself being drawn towards him until she could see his face again. He was smiling, mouth crooked. 'One can't be too choosy in this country,' he mocked.

'A typical April,' she smiled, tensely joining him in the small joke.

'Thick mists and heavy ground frost,' he sighed as he pulled her gently beneath the warm crook of his arm. 'Not Boston, hmm?'

'No,' Madeline agreed. 'Not Boston.'

'Come on.' He hugged her closer, leading her to the big black bulk which was the old boathouse, having to lean his full weight against the creaky old door to get it to open.

His smile when he turned it on her was full of rueful whimsy. 'Welcome to my humble abode,' he drawled, offering her a mocking bow. 'Please step this way, ma'am.'

'Oh!' She gasped in surprise as she stepped inside and saw the light from a flickering oil lamp hanging from the old oak rafters, lighting the thick red blanket spread out on the boarded floor. On top stood a bottle and two fluted wine glasses. 'Charming,' she complimented, pulling off her warm woollen gloves and shoving them into the pockets of her thick sheepskin coat. 'Champagne?' she quizzed, wrinkling her nose at him enquiringly.

'Breakfast,' he improvised. 'Here...' Taking her arm again, he led her over to the blanket and invited her to sit down using the boathouse wall to lean against, then joined her, groaning ruefully as his sparse behind made contact with the hard floor. 'I think I'm getting too old for this!' he complained.

'But not for drinking champagne on a cold and frosty morning?'

'Oh, never too old for that, I hope.' He reached for the bottle.

The cork popped, and Madeline made a mad grab for the glasses, laughing as she held them quickly beneath the frothing wine. In minutes they were sitting huddled into their warm coats with the boathouse wall against their backs and their shoulders rubbing against each other as they drank.

'Like old times,' Dominic murmured after a while.

Madeline turned wide eyes on him; they looked larger than life because she had a black woollen hat pulled closely around her ears. 'We never actually did this before,' she said.

'Well...' He gave a small shrug, his smile warm and teasing. 'Almost like old times, then,' he amended. 'Remember the time we punted up the river and got ourselves tangled in a salmon poacher's net?'

'My,' Madeline recalled, 'but you were angry that day.' She remembered the way he had almost overturned the boat as he yanked the poacher's net out of the river.

'My, but I was,' he mocked the loose accent.

She glanced quickly at him to see if he was deriding her, then dissolved into soft laughter at his teasing expression. 'Don't be cheeky!' she scolded, then gasped when she found herself pulled across his lap, their faces very close, the teasing gone, to be replaced by something far more disturbing.

Her soft sigh fanned his face, and his did the same to hers. Without taking his eyes from hers, he lifted his glass to her lips, and Madeline drank, the bubbles fizzing on her tongue. Without having to be prompted, she offered him her glass and watched, with breathless fascination, him sip and slowly swallow.

Their eyes remained locked on one another as silently they fed each other wine, nerves beginning to tingle while they told each other things they dared not put into words. Overhead, the flickering flame from the oil lamp played across his lean features, his satin-black hair, his eyes, not hooded but lazily engrossed, his lips, wet with wine and wearing the sensual softness of a man anticipating what was to come. She smiled gently at him, and struggled to pull her hand out from where it was trapped between their warm bodies so that she could dip her finger in the champagne then stroke it across his mouth, the finger trembling as his lips trembled. Then he caught the finger in his mouth, and sucked it delicately. Her stomach turned over and secreted a warm, stinging heat to her loins. Solemnly, Dominic returned the gesture, slowly circling her parted lips with champagne before allowing her to take it into her mouth.

Her eyelids lowered, the sensation of that smooth-textured pad against her tongue holding her languid with pleasure. Then he was taking the glass from her hand, and placing them both aside, and still they remained like that, Dominic leaning against the boathouse wall, Madeline cradled on his lap, their faces close enough to read every expression on the other.

Tension began to build between them, a deliciously warm kind of tension that centred itself low down in her stomach and slowly inched its way outwards. Her pulses quickened, her breathing with it, and she felt the muscles in his thighs begin to tighten, heat fanning out from both of them.

'Madeline...' he murmured, then reached up to pull the hat from her head. Her hair tumbled down, wild and free, just how he liked it, and his hand was burrowing into the thick silken mass, cupping her head and slowly— painfully slowly bringing her mouth up against his own.

He tasted of champagne, his breath warm, face cold and clean-smelling. She found the parting in his coat and ran her hands inside it, exploring his rock-hard ribcage beneath the fleecy check he was wearing. A shaky sigh broke from him, sheer pleasure at her touch, and she sighed too, against his mouth, this kiss threatening none of the angry passion of the night before, yet just as poignant, making its own special kind of statement like a pledge.

Her head was resting in the thickly padded hollow of his shoulder by the time he drew his mouth from hers. 'I'm not going to seduce you here,' he said quietly, reaching inside his coat to capture one of her hands so that he could tangle his own fingers with hers, bringing it up to kiss her knuckles one by one. 'And it would be a seduction if I were crude enough to make love to you here, on a cold bed of wood and coarse blanket.' His eyes ran intently over her face, for once completely free of the sophisticated masks it usually wore these days. 'It will be a soft bed and silk sheets for you, Madeline, my love,' he promised huskily. 'But I'm going to touch you,' he added darkly, 'touch you and caress you until you can't think of any other man but me. And not because of any barbaric desire to inflict my own will on you, but because I just can't help myself.'

He covered her mouth with his own again, slowly, luxuriously almost, deepening the kiss, and Madeline let him move at his own pace, too aware of the times before when she had inflicted her needs on to him. His hands drifted inside her coat, fingers lightly feathering along her blouse until they found her breasts, and she let out a soft sigh of satisfaction as he began stroking lightly.

Their coats formed a warm cocoon around them, their mouths drinking deeply of each other. Outside the birds were just beginning to waken, their spasmodic bursts of song barely impinging on the cosy little world inside the boathouse. A horse whinnied, its bridle jingling as it tossed its head, and the kiss broke reluctantly apart.

'More,' she demanded, not even bothering to open her eyes, her kiss-moistened lips parted and ready.

'Patience,' he admonished, and shifted their position, gently laying her down on the blanket so that he could lean over her, and he began parting the buttons of her shirt. She shivered as the cold air hit her exposed skin, bringing her lashes flickering upwards to find him gazing at her with black burning eyes.

'No bra,' he said.

'Not for you,' she answered, bringing his gaze up to clash with hers.

It was such a telling admission, one which sent a light tremor rippling across his resting body. Unbreathing, they gazed at each other for a long beautiful moment, feeling and allowing the tension to build between them until it played like static on the surface of their skin.

Then his eyes were back on her breasts, those thick curling lashes of his fanning his cheeks as he studied her lazily, the full firm mounds with their darkened circles and hard, tight, inviting nubs trembling a little as they moved in rhythm with her quickened breathing.

His own shirt parted quicker than hers had, his fingers fumbling with the buttons and dragging the two pieces of fleecy cloth apart to expose his own deeply tanned and muscle-packed chest covered in a thick covering of crisp black hair.

Features taut now with the control he was forcing on himself, he came over her and lowered his naked chest on to hers. Tiny darts of pleasure shot out in all directions, making her gasp and him groan.

'Wonderful,' he sighed, and she watched with an inner thrill his lashes close over his eyes in pleasurable response. 'You have no idea how much I've wanted to do this,' he murmured thickly, burying his face in her warm throat, 'feel your skin against my own.'

'You said no seduction,' she reminded him.

'Trust me,' he urged. 'I know what I'm doing.'

His eyes closed again. Madeline watched the taut sensual line of his mouth soften, part and turn slightly to cover hers, and allowed her own eyes to close. Dominic knows what he's doing, her brain chanted soothingly to her, and curled her hands inside his shirt. As the kiss deepened, her hand had already found the tight male nipples nestling in their bed of crisp black hair...

Her head was resting on his arm, cushioned from the hardness of the wooden floor. Their breathing becoming more laboured as the minutes ticked by. They could have been all alone in the world for all it mattered. Just the two of them, with Dominic caressing her breasts with the light pleasing touch of his hands, one jeans-clad thigh pressed between her own and moving in a slow tormenting rhythm along her inner thigh.

Several times they stopped kissing just to gaze at each other. No words; they didn't seem necessary. As Dominic had said, he was in control of things. This was no seduction, just a beautiful loving they had shared many times in the past. Often here, by the river, sometimes in his apartment above the bank. Soon he would stop, as he always had, before things got really out of hand. Soon he would begin to withdraw, gently soothe her back to earth with his hands and his mouth, murmuring the same words she still recalled from years ago. 'We have to stop now, we have to stop.' The chant played languorously in her mind. 'We have to stop....'

But he didn't stop. Quite when Dominic had lost control of the situation she wasn't sure, but it was the zip sliding down on her jeans that alerted her to the fact that he was taking this further than he had ever done four years ago.

'Dominic?' she whispered uncertainly.

'It's all right,' he assured her tightly. 'I just want to touch you, Madeline. I need to...' The words trailed away on a broken sigh as he eased the jeans away from her hips and slid his hand between her thighs.

Lightning struck the throbbing core of her being, sending her into a convulsion of gasps. And suddenly he wasn't so slow and languid, but tight with urgency, his mouth hard on her own, his skin burning hot where he pressed down upon her, his fingers drawing a cry from her as she felt her body quicken, become engulfed in wild liquid heat, and she was thrown into a spiralling world she had never visited before, tumbling down and down with no control over herself or the feelings rocketing through her.

She cried out his name in sheer fright, her fingers clinging to him, nails digging into the sweat-sheened skin at his shoulders. She heard him mutter something, then those tormenting fingers sent her flying over the edge while he leaned over her, watching the rapturous torture convulse her body, his eyes bright and black with impassioned triumph.

When it was over, he pulled her to him, cradling her against the warmth of his body, rocking her to and fro as if she were a baby in dire need of comfort.

'My God,' she gasped when she found the air to do it. 'Why?' Bewilderment threaded her tone, her eyes wide and staring at the rickety old ceiling above their heads. He rolled away from her, covering his eyes with his arm, but Madeline could see the self-contempt in the tight line around his mouth.

'I'm sorry,' he muttered.

'Sorry!' She sat up, dizzy with the drunken aftermath of what he had just done to her, and confused as to why he had done it. 'Dominic—what was the difference between what you've just done and making love to me properly?' she demanded in a strangled tone.

'You're still a virgin.'

'I'm—what?' Anger surged up from nowhere, brought on, she suspected, by the sheer shock of what had just

taken place. 'Y-you mean you've just put me through—
that—because you think I'm still a virgin?'

That brought his arm away from his eyes, the guarded
look in them overlaid by a sharp question. His face was
pale, the tension in him clenching his lean frame.

Madeline climbed to her feet, her body trembling as
she angrily straightened her clothing. Humiliation and
embarrassment stung along her body; she had never felt
so ill-used in all her life!

'You used to hate it when I stopped too soon before,'
he explained. 'I didn't want to disappoint you this time.'

'And what you did just now was supposed to make
me feel better, was it?' She sent him a bitter glance, 'Well,
let me tell you how I really feel,' she muttered on a burst
of fury which had been building over four long frustrating years. 'I feel used! Used and manipulated! As I
always did when I was with you!'

'Madeline, I——'

'I want to be loved, not relieved!' she choked. Tears
were burning at the back of the throat and her eyes and
she looked away from him. 'Loved, and wanted so desperately that you wouldn't be able to stop no matter how
hard you tried!'

'I didn't want to stop,' he put in gruffly.

'But managed it anyway.' The short laugh was more
a cry of scorn as she fumbled to do up her shirt buttons
with fingers that trembled badly. 'As always,' she went
on self-condemningly, 'it's Dominic who plays the tune
and Madeline who dances to it!' she scoffed at herself,
then shuddered in sickening self-disgust. 'You always did
only have to touch me to have me panting for more,
didn't you?' she accused him and viciously mocked
herself.

'It wasn't like that,' he sighed out wearily, sitting up
to run an angry hand through his hair. 'It was never like

that. You were so young then, Madeline! Just eighteen, dammit!'

'And now?' she challenged shakily. 'What am I now, Dom—four years older and therefore eligible for the next stage in sexual titillation?'

'Don't be so damned crude,' he grunted, lurching grimly to his feet. 'You enjoyed what we just shared, Madeline, and you know it.'

'But we didn't "share" anything!' she cried, the tears spurting to her eyes again on a fresh burst of anger and ravished pride. 'We never did "share", and that's just my point! You manipulated me to suit your own ends four years ago and you're still trying to manipulate me now!'

Four years ago he had held her on a knife-edge of mind-blasting sexual frustration with his clever hot-and-cold tactics. Then, when she'd inevitably toppled over the edge, he'd had the absolute gall to be appalled by her! And this morning he had done the exact same thing, fooling her into that mad, crazy, beautiful experience only to blow cold on her yet again.

She couldn't stand it. Not again. She should not have come back. She should never have set foot inside England again until she'd worked Dominic Stanton right out of her system with however many lovers as it would have taken to do it! But instead she'd held them all off, and secretly dreamed of Dom, of his touch of her skin, of his kisses and caresses.

God, she felt sick. Sick with herself and with him. 'I don't wish to see you again,' she said as she pulled her thick coat around her. 'Not in this way, anyway.' Her gaze did a cynical run of the old boathouse. 'You aren't good for me, Dominic. You rob me of my self-respect. You always did.'

'And what do you think you did to me?' he threw back harshly.

'I made a fool of you,' she said. 'And do you know what?' she added. 'For the first time in four years of feeling guilty about it, I've just come the conclusion that you damned well deserved it!'

CHAPTER TEN

'EVERYONE has accepted,' Nina remarked from the elegant secretaire where she sat shuffling through the replies to her wedding invitations. 'Including all the Stantons,' she added with smiling satisfaction.

'And so they should,' Edward Gilburn gruffed, 'considering the way you went over there and flannelled around them all.'

'I did not flannel!' Nina protested. 'I just thought it was best to give them all their invitations personally since they had to know that everyone else received theirs weeks ago.'

'And very right it was, too,' Louise put in, soothing her daughter's ruffled feathers.

'Did you see Dom?' Madeline couldn't resist asking the question, but hated herself for doing it.

But she hadn't seen or heard from him since that awful scene at the boathouse over a week ago now. And the pained sense of loss she was experiencing felt as desperate as it had done four years ago.

'Dom said he would be delighted to come to my wedding,' Nina answered her.

Madeline waited, with bated breath, hoping that Nina was going to tell her that Dom asked after her, but she added nothing else, and on a sudden fit of restlessness she got up and walked over to stare out of the window. When she'd told Dom they were no good for each other, she had been right, she decided. These awful feelings at wretchedness were just not worth it.

'Did you know old Major Courtney passed away last year, Maddie?' her father said suddenly.

'No!' she gasped, turning around to stare at him. Major Courtney had been the local recluse, living in his tumble-down old house for as far back as Madeline could remember. The house and the man fitted together somehow. It didn't seem right that he would be there no longer.

'So who's living in the house now?' she asked, oddly resenting the idea of anyone else but the major being there.

Her father shrugged. 'Nobody in their right mind,' he scoffed. 'It was common knowledge that none of his relatives wanted to live there. After all, they didn't give a hoot about the old major or his house. But someone seems to have taken it over—although it never actually came on the open market,' he added thoughtfully. 'There have been builders in there for months now doing it up. You wouldn't know it, Maddie,' he said. 'It's had a new roof, and all the black and white wooden facers have been renovated. Whoever it is who's bought the place, they're spending a small fortune on it—fools. I wouldn't want to live there if you paid me to!'

I would, Madeline thought yearningly. I would have loved to buy the place and bring it back to its former glory—make it look just like that picture she'd seen hanging in Dominic's den. She let out a soft sigh, turning back to stare out of the window at the bleak cold day beyond. Years ago, when she and Dom had been a pair, she'd used to make him drive past just so she could gaze at the crumbling old place. Why she felt this affinity with it she'd never really understood.

'I bet ghosts go around it clanging rusty old chains with their heads tucked underneath their arms.' She heard her own voice, filled with relish, echo back at her through the years.

'While ladies in miserable grey robes go sailing mournfully by?' Dom had suggested mockingly.

'Why not?' she'd pouted, then quivered expressively. 'Mmm, what a lovely atmosphere to live in!'

'You gruesome creature,' Dom had exclaimed.

'I may take a walk over there this afternoon,' she pondered out loud.

It would give her something to do. This last week had seemed endless. Endless—endless...

'Missing Perry already?' her father remarked, completely misreading the wistful sound in her voice.

Perry had returned to Boston a couple of days ago, not even trying to hide his disappointment in her. 'You didn't even put up a fight against him,' he'd accused her. 'He just crooked his little finger and you went running.' He'd seen her ride out that misty morning, and heard her return telling hours later. 'What has the man got that makes you so easy for him?'

My heart, she answered now, though she'd given no excuse to Perry. There hadn't been one. He was right and she had made it easy for Dom.

'Perry and I are just friends, Daddy,' she answered a little irritably. 'Good, close friends, but that's all.'

'Then it must be Boston you're missing,' he decided, studying her from beneath thoughtfully lowered brows. 'Because we certainly don't seem to be providing whatever it is you need to make you happy here.'

Quietly, with a nod at her daughter and a sympathetic glance at her husband, Louise got up and left the room with Nina.

'I'm fine,' Madeline said, hearing the other two go with a rueful little smile playing about her lips because she knew just what their exit meant. They'd all had

enough of her moping aimlessly about the place, and
her father meant to get to the bottom of the reason for
it. So she took in a deep breath and turned to smile at
him. 'It isn't Boston, or Perry that's bothering me,' she
assured him. 'It's just that I feel . . .' What did she feel?
she wondered helplessly.

That was it, she realised with a grimace. She felt
helpless. Helplessly in love and helplessly—helpless to
do anything about it.

'You know what you need?' her father said, eyeing
her sagely. 'You need something to fill up your time. In
Boston you worked in that interior design place Dee
spends all her money in—what was it called?'

'Shackles,' she provided with a small smile because
he was looking disapproving, and not because his darling
daughter had taken herself a job, but simply because
poor Dee had got her that job instead of himself.

'Stupid name for a shop,' he muttered. 'But,' his eyes
lit up with a sudden idea, 'there's no reason why you
couldn't find a similar post here—or even better,' he
added, leaning forwards in his chair with enthusiasm.
'We could set you up with an interior design shop of
your own, right here in Lambourn—or Reading if you
prefer!'

Her dark head shook apologetically. 'You need some
formal training to set up a place like that, Daddy. I'm
just not qualified to open up my own place.'

'Only because you pulled back from going to art
college because of Dominic Stanton,' he said with gruff
censure. 'But that doesn't mean you haven't got it in
you to do the job! Or, if it comes to that, go to university and get your degree now!' Her expression brought
the gleam of challenge to his eyes. 'Why not?' he demanded. 'You got good grades in your A levels, and you
wouldn't be the only student to take on further edu-

cation several years late! Why not, Maddie?' he insisted
when she still looked reluctant. 'There is nothing to stop
you after all!'

Nothing at all, she agreed, turning away again so that
he wouldn't see the depression weighing heavily on her
features as her thoughts went inevitably back to Dom.
Finding herself still vulnerable to Dominic had put a stop
to any idea she might have had of remaining here in
England.

'I'll think about it,' she offered as a salve. 'After the
wedding. I'll think about it then.'

'Maddie, dear . . .' It was only as he spoke that she
realised her father had got up from his chair and come
to stand beside her. 'Is it still Dominic Stanton?' he
asked, oh, so gently.

Tears spurted into her eyes, and she blinked, unable
to answer, even though she was desperate to offer a reassuring no.

'We were all so damned pleased when you two got
together four years ago!' he sighed out heavily. 'And I
know we all have our own bit of blame to carry around
for the way we pushed you both at each other. Louise
warned me—she warned all of us that we should leave
you alone and give you time to explore your feelings for
each other. But we—James Stanton and I—we
were——'

'Daddy.' Madeline turned, placing her fingers over his
lips to stop him, her eyes bright with unshed tears.
'Please don't,' she whispered. 'I love you very dearly,
but please—please don't?'

His sigh was warm and shaky against her resting
fingers, then he was gathering her into his arms and
hugging her in the same way he had done all her life.

'Go for your walk,' he suggested gruffly after a
moment. 'It will help clear your head.'

She was standing in the hall pulling on her sheepskin coat when the telephone in the study began to ring, she heard her father's voice answer, and was just turning away when his head popped around the study door.

'Oh,' he said, sounding faintly disconcerted, almost disappointed that she was actually there. 'I caught you, then. It's—it's for you,' he informed her gruffly. 'Dominic,' he added, cleared his throat, hesitated a moment longer than walked off briskly down the hall toward Louise's private sitting-room while Madeline stared blankly after him.

She found her feet dragging as she went into the study and closed the door. The plain buff receiver lay off its rest on her father's desk, his gold-rimmed spectacles lying at right angles to it.

Dom was on the phone was all she could think, staring down at it. Dom was on the phone and wanted to speak to her.

Her hand was trembling as she picked up the receiver and carried it to her ear. 'Hello?' she murmured, then closed her eyes while she waited for the seductive beauty of his voice to wash over her.

There was a pause, as though he was no longer certain he wanted to speak to her, and her heart began to thump heavily in her breast. 'Dominic?' she whispered promptingly, having to bite down hard on her bottom lip to stop herself begging him not to ring off.

God, she thought wretchedly. This is awful! Much much worse than it had been the first time around. She was shaking all over, even her knees were trembling, like her breath as it left her agitated lungs.

'I want to see you,' he said, and the husky tone in his voice told her he was finding this just as difficult as she was. 'I've been away,' he added quickly. 'I only got back an hour ago or I would have rung sooner. Will you meet me somewhere this afternoon?'

'I...I was just on my way out, actually,' she said, saying the first thing that came into her head because the relief at hearing his voice was so violent that she'd gone light-headed with it.

'Linburgh's gone back to Boston,' he stated curtly, as though he believed Perry was the only reason she would ever step out of the house.

'Did I say otherwise?' she asked, blinking in bewilderment.

'Will he be coming back?'

'I... Well...' She frowned, not seeing the relevance of the question. 'Not until Nina's wedding, no,' she answered honestly. 'But I don't see what Perry's movements have to do with——'

'I would say they have a lot to do with everything,' he cut in gruffly. 'I have something for you, something I promised you once. Will you meet me, Madeline?'

Something he'd promised her? Her frown deepened as she tried to think what in heaven's name it could be? 'Where?' she asked, and closed her eyes again in the hopes that doing so would shut out Perry's voice telling her how easy she made it for Dom. 'He just crooked his little finger', he'd said. And he was right.

'Were you about to go anywhere special?' he countered curiously.

'Just for a walk,' she admitted. 'I was on my way to take a look at the old Courtney place. My father has been telling me that someone is having the old place renovated, and I thought I would like to take a last look at it before it changes beyond all recognition.'

There was a short silence, then, 'It's a bit early in the year to go crab-appling, isn't it, Madeline?' Dominic murmured softly.

Despite the tension in her she had to smile at that. In her young day, she'd used to find nothing more exciting than making secret forays into the major's orchard to steal from his overgrown and neglected fruit tree. It wasn't the fruit that drew her there, but the sheer exhilaration in knowing that if the old man caught her he would think nothing of threatening her with his loaded shotgun. He had never actually fired it, of course, but in those days she had been impressionable enough to believe he might.

'You, of course, were never young,' she mocked him drily.

'Once,' he confessed wistfully. 'A long, long time ago before a black-haired witch with dangerously alluring eyes cast her wicked spells on me and turned me into a very old man.'

The growing smile began to ease some of the strain out of her face. 'Have you any idea who bought the house?'

'Haven't heard anything on the grapevine,' he answered. 'Are you riding, or driving?'

'Walking, actually,' she informed him a little defensively, knowing she was revealing more of her present mood than she would like. April was being its usual seasonal self and blowing up crisp cold winds from the north which were likely to bring rain with them, the dark clouds rolling in from nowhere to drop their icy load before rolling onwards again. And Dom would be well aware that she had decided to walk simply because she couldn't resist battling with the unpredictable elements.

'I'll meet you there in about an hour, then,' he said, and put down the phone.

Madeline stared at it, wondering pensively just what she was doing agreeing to meet him when she knew it would bring her nothing but pain. Then she happened to glance sideways at the mirror hanging above the old marble fireplace, and she knew why she had agreed. It was all there in her face, shining like a damned beacon for anyone to read if they wished to. Her eyes were glowing, her mouth had taken on an upward curl, and she felt happy, alive for the first time in over a week. And that was why she was going to meet him, because he was the only person on this earth who could make her feel like this.

Dominic's car wasn't anywhere to be seen when she arrived in the driveway to Courtney Manor, and she paused, gazing along the tree-lined driveway to where the old house stood, still looking charmingly rickety despite the amount of work which had obviously been done to it already. As her father had said, the roof had been completely replaced, and the black and white facer beams no longer wore the yellow-grey tinge of age and neglect. The rustic bricks, too, had been neatly repointed, and the tall chimney stacks had been straightened out. Madeline tipped her head to one side in an effort to put them back as she remembered them.

'There was a crooked man who bought a crooked house,' she murmured softly to herself, recalling the time she had chanted the rhyme at Dominic.

The wind gusted suddenly, blowing her long hair across her face, and she had to take a hand out of her coat pocket to push it away again, her gaze darting up to one of the upper diamond-leaded windows when she thought she'd caught a glimpse of a face there. But there was no one. Could it be haunted? Her eyes skimmed the upper windows once again but saw nothing, and her smile went awry. She always could think herself into a state of high drama for no other reason than because she enjoyed it.

No self-respecting ghost would even want to haunt this house in the state it was in now!

She began walking down the drive, eyeing with some deep inner pleasure she had never been able to explain the small-framed leaded windows with their thick black-painted wooden lintels above and below them. The front porch had a new shiny coat of black paint on it, its high-pitched slate-covered roof built at the same steep angle as the main roof to the house. It was supposed to be empty, and there were signs that major work was still in progress in the several types of heavy machinery standing idle in the drive, but she could just make out what appeared to be curtains hanging at some of the windows, and whoever had bought the place was obviously very close to moving in.

Hands dug deep into her coat pockets, she moved closer until she was standing in front of the deep porch, and let her curious gaze skim slowly over the downstairs windows before she decided that, since she had come this far, it couldn't hurt to take a tiny peek inside a few of them. Moving cautiously, tentatively almost, she stepped on to the newly turned flowerbed just below the closest window and peered inside.

It was impossible to tell what kind of room it was since the light today was not very good and the tiny windows had not been designed to let much light in, but there was just enough light to tell her that, far from being ready for habitation, the inside of Courtney Manor had a long way to go yet.

Stepping back, she began walking slowly around the house, pausing to peer into each window as she reached it. Around the back, the garden was still overgrown and wild. Once upon a time there would have been a well stocked kitchen garden here, then the orchard beyond it leading right down to the edge of the river, but it had all become so badly overgrown now that it was impossible to tell where garden finished and the orchard began.

The old coach house and stable block appeared barely touched as yet, and she guessed by the huge padlock chained to the doors that the builders must be using them as storerooms for now.

The back door was big and old, reached by several cracked and very worn steps, to one side of which were the moss-covered steps to the basement. The windows here were too high for her to see through, so after a wistful scan of the rear view of the house she made her way around the front again, feeling an odd heaviness of heart as she paused there for a final long look.

'Try the door if you like. It is unlocked.'

Madeline yelped, fright rippling along her spine as she spun around to stare in the direction the voice had come from.

Dom stood just a few yards away from her, his dark hair blowing in the strong wind.

'What a stupid thing to do!' she cried, anger flaring with the sudden rush of adrenalin to her system.

'Did you think I was the major's ghost?' he grinned, not in the least bit penitent.

'Where did you come from?' she asked, glancing around in search of his car.

'It isn't here,' he murmured, correctly guessing what she was looking for.

It was only as her eyes came back to him that she realised that he was not wearing a coat. In fact, he was standing there in just black trousers and a thin white shirt. It hit her then with a disturbing thud.

'It's your house, isn't it?' she said. 'You're the one who's bought this place.'

He sent her a mocking little smile then let his eyes drift away from hers to run over the improved frontage of his latest purchase. The wind was getting stronger, rippling the thin fabric of his shirt against his chest, disturbing the cluster of black hair at the open V where the buttons were left casually undone.

He looked oddly very alone standing there like that, with his shoulders hunched slightly against the cold and his hands pushed into the pockets of his trousers. The cold was etching out the strong bone-structure of his face, paling his skin a little, making his hair appear blacker, his eyes darker.

'It looks like rain,' he murmured suddenly, returning his gaze to her. Then slowly, uncertainly almost, he lifted a hand towards her. 'Let's go inside,' he suggested gruffly, 'and I'll show you around.'

A fleeting vision of how that outstretched hand had last touched her came shuddering into her mind and she had to close her eyes on the violent upsurge of feeling she experienced, her own hands clenching tightly in the pockets of her sheepskin coat, shame at her own wanton behaviour drawing in the corners of her downturned mouth.

'Come on.' Suddenly he was beside her, the hand gentle on her arm, and she opened her eyes to find him standing right in front of her, his taut expression telling her that he knew exactly where her thoughts had taken her off to. 'Come on,' he repeated, low and gruff, and the hand slid up to her shoulders, drawing her close into the side of his body as he turned them towards the front door of the house.

They entered together, Dom moving only slightly away from her so that he could close the door behind them, shutting the sharp cold wind outside—and closing them in.

Met by the sudden silence, Madeline stood very still with Dom's arm warm about her shoulders. She was barely breathing, her senses tuned exclusively in to him, and she had to force herself to take in her surroundings.

They were standing in a large square hallway on a very old stone-flagged floor which would probably once have been the main room of the house where an Elizabethan family would have eaten off a huge refectory table, and sat in the evening by a blazing log fire set in the grate of an enormous stone and timber fireplace which almost completely dominated the central wall of the house.

It would have been cold and draughty, and, with the wind blowing from a certain direction, probably engulfed in smoke from the fire. But it was all here in this big almost ugly reception hall—the history, the sheer romantic excitement of wild and wicked Elizabethan living. And Madeline knew that if she closed her eyes she would be able to summon up the ghostly apparitions of swash-buckling men, and women draped in velvet and ermine laughing and joking, uncaring of the discomfort of their surroundings, their voices ringing against the solid stone walls and up the heavy wooden staircase which hugged another wall, curving up to the galleried landing above.

'There is a crystal chandelier to go back up there,' Dominic said beside her, noting the way she was staring up at the age-blackened beams of solid oak which spanned the crudely plastered ceiling. 'It was so filthy that we didn't know what a treasure we had until we got it down. Superb thing,' he murmured with quiet satisfaction. 'It's being professionally cleaned and restored at the moment—along with a whole lot of other old treasures we discovered beneath the centuries of dust once we began looking.'

'Poor major,' Madeline murmured sadly. 'If everything was in such a poor state—how did he live with it?'

'Sheer cussedness, I should imagine,' Dom said with a wry smile, then, 'Actually, the few rooms he seemed to use in the house were all kept in a surprisingly pristine condition. The library, for instance.' He moved away from Madeline to go and open a door to their left. 'He seemed to live, eat and sleep in here, poring over his old books and papers—most of them military. They, like everything else in the house, have been taken away to be restored and valued.'

Madeline was frowning as she went to join him at the open door, her footsteps echoed on the cold flagged floor as she went to join him at the entrance to a big, surprisingly well lit room literally lined with empty bookshelves. 'But surely the Courtney family would have emptied the place of anything valuable before you bought it from them? I mean,' she murmured in puzzlement, 'if some of the stuff in here is as old as you say, it must be worth a fortune!'

Dom just shrugged. 'I offered them a good price for the lot,' he informed her dismissively. 'And they—indifferent fools that they were—accepted it. Morons, the lot of them.' His derision was obvious. 'It's no wonder the major had nothing to do with them. They cared nothing for the old man or his belongings. And all they wanted was the best price they could get to have the whole thing taken off their hands. I gave it them and they accepted it. It was their loss and my gain.'

'Speaks the hardened banker,' Madeline mocked his dismissive shrug.

'Speaks a man who abhors neglect, whether it be of a human being or his possessions,' he corrected. 'By the time I've finished with this place, it will look exactly as it would have done if the old man and his house had not been left to rot alone.'

Looking up at him, Madeline saw that the mask of disgust was tinged with something else she couldn't quite recognise. 'And you'll enjoy filling it with all those weird and wonderful curiosities you've been gathering about you all your life.'

That brought a crooked smile to his face. 'Of course. This house is the ideal setting for them, don't you think? Come on.' He reached for her hand. 'I'll show you the rest of the place.

The house was much larger than it looked from the outside, with an interesting hotchpotch of oddly shaped rooms all with at least one outstanding feature to fire Madeline's artistic mind into action, and within minutes they were discussing how best to decorate and furnish without spoiling the period flavour of the house. The work still in progress on the ground floor was extensive, but as they moved up to the first floor Madeline could see that up here was almost ready for habitation.

'We've been working from the top down,' Dominic explained. 'And the workmen moved off this floor only last week—which is why we keep the doors up here all tightly closed.' He reached out to open one of them and stepped inside, drawing her with him. 'Though this is the only room that's completely finished. The master bedroom,' he announced with an oddly mocking little bow.

'Oh!' she gasped in surprise, moving away from him to go and stand in the centre of a thick-piled dusky-pink carpet. Her eyes were wide with surprise as she turned in a slow circle, so shocked that she didn't know what to say, his colour choice in here nothing like she would ever have expected a man like him to choose.

The room was dominated by a ceiling-canopied four-poster bed built of rich mahogany and draped with heavy silver and dusky pink brocade. It was huge, outrageously flamboyant in the way the brocade looped and twisted its way around the thick wood frame. The mattress itself was covered in a reverse match of the same fabric, its size alone enough to intimidate, and she glanced jerkily away from it to stare at the incredibly ornate mahogany fireplace that took up almost all of the wall opposite.

The room was big—big enough also to accommodate two big and comfy-looking armchairs flanking the fireplace, again upholstered with a matching blend brocade, like the windows and the several lamps dotted about.

'Well,' Dominic prompted when she had stood there for a good long minute without uttering a single sound, 'what do you think?'

Think? A hard lump formed in her throat. It was a beautiful room. But a room so obviously designed to share with a woman he must love deeply that she felt the lump melt into tears and had to turn away from the intense expression on his face, so that he wouldn't see just how deeply she was affected. This room was suggesting so much—so very much that she was actually afraid of what would come next.

A silence fell, throbbing tensely in the air between them, and, unable to stand it, she made to turn away towards the window, only then she saw it, the gold-framed painting hanging above the fireplace, and her body shivered to a breathless stop.

'I promised to give this to you once, remember?' He came to stand close behind her. 'The painting recently, and the house a long, long time ago, when your dreams were . . . well, just dreams and I was happy to play along with them. Well . . .' His hands came upon her shoulders, fingers closing gently, warming her all the way through to her very heart. 'The painting—the house. They're both yours, Madeline. My gift to you.'

'Oh, Dom,' she whispered thickly. 'I can't take . . .'

Suddenly his arms were around her, stopping her words and crushing her body as he hugged her tightly to him. 'Once, what seems a lifetime ago now,' he murmured, his deep tone throbbing with an emotion she felt echoing inside herself, 'a beautiful and enchanting creature I loved very much offered herself to me with all the passion in her loving nature, and I, fool that I was, turned her down.'

A hand jerked to her mouth to muffle the sob which leapt to her throat, and Dominic sighed unsteadily. 'Wild, Madeline,' he remembered gruffly. 'My God, you were wild then. I hardly knew if I was standing on my head or my feet most of the time. And I wanted you so desperately that it took every bit of my control to keep things as light as I did. And even that was taking things dangerously close to the edge.' The sob escaped and he bent to brush his mouth across her cheek. 'You were very young, my darling. And everyone kept telling me how lucky I was, and teasing me about how I was going to handle the wild and wilful baggage you were then. No one bothered asking how I was going to handle myself!' His harsh sigh vibrated against her resting spine. 'Every time I so much as looked at you my heart flipped over!'

'Dom——' She tried to cut in on him, her own voice thick with tears, but he wouldn't let her.

'Let me say it all,' he insisted. 'I wanted you so badly, Madeline, I was tormented by the need. But there they all were, all those pleased and interested people, reminding me of how young you were, advising me to take care with you, remember your age, your sweet, sweet innocence, warning me not to break that wonderful spirit of yours with too much too soon!' Another sigh ripped from him. 'Then there were the others,' he went on. 'The ones who questioned the wisdom of marrying myself to someone so young and headstrong. The ones who questioned whether you were old enough actually to know your true feelings for me—and they made me question it myself, forced me into an agony of wondering whether I was being fair to you to trap you into marriage when you'd barely even tasted life to be really sure of what you wanted from it—or from me come to that.'

'I knew,' she whispered.

His smile was sensed rather than seen. 'I could have been just another new and exciting experience to you, Madeline,' he suggested grimly. 'You have to remember how your life then was full of the need to try out new things. I began to worry that once I'd let you learn all I could teach you about love and loving you would need to be off, finding something else to soothe that frighteningly restless spirit of yours... What I'm trying to say to you, Madeline, is that I didn't dare risk making love to you before we married because I was so afraid it would mean my losing you!'

'You didn't trust my love.'

'No,' he admitted.

'And so lost me anyway.'

'Yes,' he sighed, then turned her around to face him, his eyes dark and sombre as he studied her upturned face. 'Well, now the tables are turned, and it's for me to do the offering and your chance to refuse me. If I kiss you now, and pick you up and carry you over to that big bed over there with the deliberate intention of making love to you, will you have me, Madeline?'

The silence hummed between them, tension springing along her nerve ends to hold her mute and still. Dominic looked down at her with a dark intensity which told her how absolutely serious he was, yet still she hesitated. The old Madeline would have thrown her arm around him by now, giving him his answer with kisses and wild ecstatic cries. But this Madeline had learned the art of caution, and rarely stepped into anything without being absolutely sure of its outcome.

'You want me, you know you do,' he muttered huskily when she still said nothing, her blue eyes full of her uncertainty. 'We're both four years older, Madeline. And if those four years have taught me anything besides misery and loneliness and self-contempt, then they've taught me that love, true love, endures any span of time. I love you, Madeline,' he stated solemnly. 'I think I probably always have. I know I always will. Will you please let me show you just how much?'

His voice broke and Madeline trembled, her pale face crumbling with emotion as she fell into his arms. 'Oh, Dom!' she choked. 'I missed you so!'

'Thank God.' He caught her tightly to him.

Their mouths fused and within seconds they were lost in each other. No more words, no gentle patience, the fierceness of their hunger taking them towards the big waiting bed on steps punctuated with powerful kisses and mad flurries of activity as they took the clothes from each other's bodies.

By the time Dominic pushed her down on the bed and followed her, they were naked and trembling with eagerness. Only once did he moderate his desire to a more controllable level, when their bodies, hot and burning, drenched in the sweat of love, were ready to join, and he eased himself away a little and caught her restless face in his hands, demanding she look at him.

'Pain and pleasure, Madeline,' he said thickly, his eyes black with passion and nostrils flaring at the control he was placing on himself. 'It has to be.'

'You know I haven't——?'

'You couldn't. I couldn't. We belong to each other.' And as she trembled at the full meaning of his words, he lowered his mouth back to hers, and slowly began the ultimate thrust of his hips which would unite their bodies.

He caught her soft cry of pain with his mouth, savouring it, holding her still beneath him until he felt her tension begin to wane, then he was moving fiercely, the moment of temperance gone and the full violence of their shared passion driving them to the ultimate victory, a mutual shattering of everything earthly, leaving only the spirit, stripped and vulnerable to attack. It was a woman's right to yield to the superior strength of her man—and a man's karma to have his very soul laid bare to the woman he impregnated with his need.

CHAPTER ELEVEN

MADELINE was over by the window, watching the rain pour from a storm-blackened sky, the wind lashing it against the leaded glass almost obliterating the view beyond.

Dom lay watching her from the bed, the sheet drawn down low on his hips, his body still languid from the slumber he had just woken from. His eyes were lazily enjoying the picture she presented, dressed only in his discarded shirt, her long legs bare, and her hair, that wonderful glory of black silk he so loved to smother himself in, rippling down her back in a tangle of soft glistening waves.

'What's so interesting out there?' he questioned after a while.

'Rain, rain and more rain,' she sighed, still staring outwards. 'I do hope it improves before Nina's wedding.'

'It will,' he assured with all the optimism of a true Englishman. 'Come back here to me, Madeline,' he held out his hand to her. 'I'm missing you.'

She hesitated only a moment before going to curl herself up against the warmth of his muscled body. She tucked her head into the warmth of his throat and Dominic's arms closed comfortably around her.

'I love you,' he said softly.

'I know.' She placed a kiss on his throat, but her mood was subdued, brooding, her arms folded tightly across her shirt-covered breasts.

'Hey!' Dom lifted his head from the pillow to frown at her, her strange tone making his heart miss a beat

167

beneath her resting cheek. 'What's the matter? What's wrong, Madeline?' he demanded brusquely.

'I wish—I wish... Oh, Dom,' she sighed, suddenly stretching up to wind her arms tightly around his neck. 'I don't want to ever leave you again! I don't want to leave this house, this room—I don't want all those people out there spoiling things for us a second time!'

'They won't,' he assured, holding her tightly to him. 'We won't let them come near us if you don't want them to!' He was frowning in angry confusion at her sudden and unexpected flight into anxiety. She was actually trembling with it, her tears damp against his throat. It hadn't occurred to him that the old Madeline was back with a vengeance, wild passions and fears alike.

'But they'll know,' she choked. 'They'll have to know, and then it will all start up again. The teasing, the interfering advice. They'll be questioning your sanity in taking me on again, and warning me not to make the same mistakes a second time! And—and then all the taunts will start, the reminiscences of how it was between us the first time around, and what fools we made of ourselves, and—and before we know it we'll be fighting instead of loving, and it will all turn sour!'

'No, it won't,' he stated grimly. 'Because we won't let it. Listen to me!' he commanded. 'We'll get married. Now, tomorrow, as soon as I can arrange it. We'll get married and lock ourselves away in this house where none of them can get at us if that's what you want!'

'Marry? You mean you actually want to marry me?' She sounded so sincerely shocked that Dominic shook her.

'Of course I want to marry you, you bloody fool!' he growled.

'You don't have to, you know,' she told him softly, beginning to smile because she was suddenly feeling warm and safe and very loved, and the old Madeline way of flipping from one emotion to another had happened again. 'I'm quite happy to be your mistress. In fact it sounds a rather exciting thing to be, a man's secret mistress.'

With a jerk, he rolled her on to her back so that he could loom angrily over her. 'And if you think I'll accept anything less than marriage from you, then you can damned well think again! And stop smiling at me like that!' he growled, his blue eyes fierce.

'Like what?' she asked, her fingers coming up to stroke sensuously at his taut cheeks.

'Like the cat who's just pinched all the cream!'

'I love you, Dominic,' she murmured huskily.

'God,' he groaned, closing his eyes against the devilment gleaming in hers. 'I must be mad, getting myself involved with a teasing little witch like you.'

'I love you,' she repeated, and drew his head down so that she could shower his angry face with kisses. 'Love you—love you—love you.'

'Witch,' he muttered. 'I thought the new Madeline didn't go in for acts of sensationalism.'

'She doesn't,' she stopped kissing him to protest.

'Then what was that little scene you've just staged if it wasn't pure old Madeline sensationalism?' he grunted.

'Who is the new Madeline?' she grinned.

'Oh, God.' Dominic threw himself back against the pillows. 'Don't tell me,' he groaned. 'The new Madeline has scuttled back into oblivion.'

'Who has?'

'The——' He groaned again. 'I almost fell for that,' he smiled ruefully.

'Here,' she soothed, coming to lean over him, 'fall for me instead,' she offered and kissed his answer away.

It was growing dark when they eventually emerged again. 'God, what time is it?' Madeline sat up with a jerk.

'Time?' Dominic mumbled lazily. 'What do you want to know the time for? We aren't going anywhere.' He reached out to pull her back down to him.

'I have to get home!' she protested. 'They'll be worrying about me. God!' she added with dramatic horror. 'I told my father I would only be out a couple of hours! Let me go, Dom!' she pleaded when his arms only tightened around her squirming body. 'He'll have a search party organised if I——'

'No, he won't.' The words were muffled against the silken warmth of her throat, and his hands were already making sensual forays which had her senses quickening. 'I rang your home just after you left and spoke to your father. I told him I would be taking you out to dinner, so they won't expect you back for ages yet.'

'And what did he say?' she asked curiously, remembering her own conversation with her father only minutes before she left the house.

'He told me not to bother if I was intending to hurt his daughter a second time. And I told him that, far from hurting her, I hoped to convince her that I only wanted to love her—then I invited him to lunch next week to discuss the financial backing he was after and he——'

'Hey,' she interrupted. 'Back up a little will you?' she commanded, managing to break free from him so that she could sit up, looking like a wanton gypsy with her hair wild about her face and shoulders and her naked breasts standing pearly white against the darkening room. 'You informed my father that you intended to start courting me again?'

His eyes, which were lazily exploring her body now lifted grimly to her face. 'I tried the courting bit four years ago, Madeline. I have no intention whatsoever of going through that torment a second time.'

'So, what did you say to him? Did you tell him you owned this house?' It was odd, but she found she didn't want anyone knowing about this place. She felt safe here, sure of herself, of Dominic, but if the outside world began encroaching again she...

'No,' he said gently, reading her mind. 'No one but you and I and the builders who are working on it know who owns it.'

She was still looking anxious, and Dominic frowned as she quietly disentangled herself from his arms and climbed out of the bed. After a moment he followed her, a formidable sight with nothing to hide the sleek-muscled lines of his beautiful body. He took her in his arm and held her close. 'Madeline,' he said slowly, 'I told your father that I still loved you, and that I thought you still loved me. I told him I wanted to pursue that hope until we were both sure of each other, and I also told him that I didn't want any interference from anyone. He understood, I think,' he grimaced. 'Because, other than the one warning, he didn't try to put me off. Then I asked him if he had found anyone willing to back his latest ideas as yet, and when he said he hadn't I invited him to lunch next week so we could discuss it. The call finished quite amicably if a little restrainedly. But I think he already had a suspicion of how things were between you and me.'

'He asked me,' she admitted, 'just before I left today if it was still you.'

'And what did you say?'

'I said nothing. I couldn't lie, and I didn't really know the truth. I was still feeling hurt you see—over what happened at the boathouse.'

'I'm sorry about that.' His arms tightened around her. 'I set out with honest intentions, but before I knew where I was at the whole thing had got out of hand and I found myself with a wildly beautiful, utterly desirable and very aroused woman in my arms. Old memories stopped me from making love to you properly, but I knew it would have been nothing short of torment to leave you suspended on that kind of sexual high.'

'And what about your own sexual high?'

He just shrugged that away as if it didn't count. 'It wasn't new to me and I could handle it. And anyway,' he took hold of her chin and lifted it so he could look ruefully into her eyes, 'I wanted to spin you out of control. At that moment, it meant more to me than my own satisfaction. It felt a bit like stamping ownership, watching you, feeling you reach a full climax at my touch.'

'And you don't think I wanted—needed to see and feel the same response from you?'

He shook his head, his expression grim. 'I didn't so much as give that thought consideration until you pointed it out, and then I just felt ashamed, because while I was still playing sexual games with you as if you were still eighteen years old you showed me with your contempt how utterly inadequate I had been in response to the real emotion between us. The love.'

'And now what?' she buried her face in his shoulder, the uncertainties of the future still there to worry them. They had come a long way since they had arrived here this afternoon, so far in fact that she didn't know how she was going to breathe if it wasn't the same air he breathed also.

As if she'd spoken the words out loud, Dominic hugged her closer to him and murmured, 'I know, darling, I know.'

And she sensed a grim resolve about him, a determination to do what was right for them this time, no matter what that meant to anyone else. 'Just trust me, hmm?'

Nina's wedding day dawned bright and clear. True to its fickle nature, April had gone out on a clash of thunder and let May arrive on a blaze of fire.

Madeline climbed out of bed and stretched lazily. The last few weeks had placed an almost intolerable strain on her, what with the wedding arrangements heating up to today's boiling point, and her trying to keep her relationship with Dominic completely secret.

'I don't want to steal any of the limelight from Nina,' she'd told him. 'It's her day, and having all those gossips tittering about you and me would spoil things for her.'

'I can accept that,' he'd agreed. 'Anyway, I rather like having a clandestine affair with you,' he murmured, his eyes glinting wickedly down at her. 'You were born to do shocking things, Madeline, and I only wish we could do the shocking things going on in my imagination right now, but I suppose we can't.'

'You suppose right,' she'd said sternly. They were, after all, dancing as circumspect friends should do among a full complement of eager gossips.

That had been last night at the big dinner Louise and her father had thrown for close friends and relatives. The Stantons had come *en masse*, visiting the Gilburns' home for the first time as friends again in four years. Madeline had seen Dominic and her father slope off into his study halfway through the evening, and they had both returned smiling.

'He signed,' Dom had murmured to her as soon as he could speak to her later. 'We're equal partners on this one... I hope that damned nose of his hasn't let him down this time, Madeline,' he added drily, 'or I just may sink with him!'

'Is it that big a risk?' She had stared at him anxiously.

'Darling,' he had drawled, 'everything your father does is a big risk—having you for a daughter being the biggest one of all,' he'd added teasingly.

'I'll get you for that one later,' she'd warned him.

'I'll look forward to it.' His eyes had gleamed in a way that brought the colour pouring into her cheeks, so she'd stalked away, and half the room had looked from her to Dominic's smiling face and speculated on what he must have said to Madeline Gilburn to make her so angry. And Madeline had smiled to herself because only she and Dominic knew that it wasn't anger burning in her cheeks but excitement, pure anticipatory excitement.

Perry had arrived back last night just before the guests started arriving, driving down with Forman, who was playing a very wary kind of love game with Vicky.

Perry had taken one look at Madeline when she met him at the door and said, 'My God, I'll kill him!'

Blushing, her blue eyes alive with happiness, she'd gone into his arms for a hug. 'It's wonderful,' she'd whispered. 'But it's a secret, so don't tell a soul!'

'Are they all blind here?' He'd scoffed at her claim of secrecy.

'And what about you and Christina?' she had enquired gently, searching his hazel eyes for a glimpse of the same glow she knew she was displaying. It hadn't been there.

'It's funny really,' he had said musingly. 'I went to see her, determined to sort things out between us no matter what it took, then found it took nothing at all because one look at her and I saw her for the shallow, selfish, spoiled if beautiful little brat she actually is and thought to myself, Hell, Linburgh, you've had a damned lucky escape!'

Madeline had laughed in delight. 'What did you do?' she'd demanded with bright-eyed curiosity.

'I got the hell out of there as fast as I could—what do you think I did?' he had scoffed. 'God, it was a close-run thing, that,' he'd shuddered.

'Come on,' she'd linked her arm through his and given it a comforting squeeze, 'what you need is a glass of good Scotch whisky and some pleasant company to revive your jaded spirit.' And she had led him into the drawing-room where all her family waited.

'I'll vote for that!' he had exclaimed heartily. 'So long as there are no scheming females in there waiting to grab me. I'm off women at the moment.'

Not that this aversion had showed during the evening. Every time Madeline had looked at him he was charming some poor female or other, and neither age nor beauty came into it!

Her smile was wry now as she moved over to the window to check the weather. It was going to be a hectic day, she predicted, but at least when it was over she could relax. She and Dominic could relax.

Dom . . . just his name was enough to set her sense quivering.

These last few weeks had been the most wonderful passionate—nerve-racking weeks of her whole life!

By eleven o'clock you could have cut the tension in the Gilburn house with a knife. Vicky had arrived in her usual flurry of energy, turning a glowering look on Forman Goulding who, with Perry, was trying his best to merge with the wallpaper in the drawing-room.

'Had a fall-out?' Madeline asked as the two girls went upstairs together.

'The horrible man accused me of flirting with Perry the other night!' her friend scowled.

'Oh,' Madeline murmured. 'And I suppose you weren't doing any such thing?'

'Of course I—was,' she confessed. 'But since Perry was flirting with just about anyone wearing a skirt, I don't see what right Forman had to deny me my turn!'

'Go to it, baby!' Madeline mockingly enthused. Vicky was so obviously head over heels in love with the big American that she had to let off steam with someone or explode. Forman Goulding was a very cool and self-contained man.

'You've no room to mock,' Vicky threw back churlishly. 'I've seen the way you drool over my brother when you think no one is watching you!'

'And how does your brother look at me?' Madeline could not resist asking.

'The same way,' Vicky shrugged. She still suspected them both of having a secret affair, and hadn't forgiven either of them for not telling her about it. 'I hope you're both very pleased with yourselves,' she added huffily.

'Oh, we are,' Madeline murmured on a soft smile.

'What's that supposed to mean?' Vicky pounced like a hungry cat.

'Madeline, can you come and help me with this damned cravat?' To her undying relief, her father appeared at the door to his room, red-faced with impatience. 'What's the use of having a wife if she's never around when a man needs her?' he muttered. 'Hello, Vicky, dear.' He stopped grumbling to smile when he saw Vicky standing next to Madeline. 'Did your father get that magazine I sent over for him?'

'Yes, thank you, Uncle Edward.' The old endearment was coming easier each time Vicky said it. She had confessed to Madeline that no matter how she tried she could not call him Mr Gilburn; the formal title just simply stuck in her throat. She had been calling him Uncle for as far back in her life as she could remember. 'He said to tell you the article was just the one he wanted to read.'

'Huh, good, yes, well…Madeline, this damned cravat tie!' he growled to hide his embarrassment.

Adults, Madeline decided as she followed him back into his room while Vicky carried on down the landing to Nina's room, adults found it much harder to heal rifts than children did!

Louise's usual calm fell apart at the seams exactly ten minutes before the car was due to take her off to the church with Perry and Forman to accompany her.

It was seeing Nina dressed in all her wedding finery that did it, and when she began sobbing into her handkerchief Madeline ushered her quickly out of the room in case she upset Nina, who had been amazingly calm until now.

'She looks like an angel!' Louise sobbed. 'A sweet little angel!'

'Which she is,' said Madeline calmingly. Then to herself—Thank God I shan't be put through all of this!

'What if Charles has changed his mind?' Louise jerked out half hysterically. 'What if he doesn't turn up at the church and leaves my baby——'

'No, Louise!' Madeline cut in sharply. 'You know that won't happen. Why, knowing Charles, he's been camping outside the church since nine this morning just to make sure he gets his prize!'

In her raw silk suit of hyacinth-blue, Louise managed a thick laugh, and, relieved to see her regaining her control, Madeline quickly led her down the stairs and handed her over to her father with an expressive glance heavenwards for deliverance when she caught Perry's amused eye.

'OK,' she said bracingly as she entered Nina's room. 'Panic over... how are you feeling, poppet?'

Not long now, she thought wearily. The strain of it all was beginning to make her head ache.

The church organ struck up a traditional bridal march and Nina stepped forward on Edward Gilburn's proud arm, her gown of softly flowing pure white silk whispering on the carpeted aisle as she went. Madeline walked behind with Vicky, their matching gowns of rich cream silk doing different things for their contrasting colouring. She spotted Dominic immediately, standing in a pew next to the aisle. He turned to smile at her just as Charles turned to smile at Nina, and as she passed slowly by him their hands brushed, fingers briefly tangling and untangling in a single smooth movement, but it was all she needed to make her glow inside, her heart swelling with happiness and contentment as she stepped forward to relieve Nina of her pretty bouquet.

'Dearly beloved, we are gathered in the sight of God...'

The wedding service began, and Madeline closed her eyes, listening to the words, silently repeating the vows, pretending to herself that this was her wedding-day, and that it were she and Dominic standing there in front of the altar having their union blessed by God.

Long, tiring hours later, Dominic came up behind her and slid his hands around her waist, drawing her gently back against him. 'How much longer before we can get out of here?'

Her hands went up to cover his where they lay against the flatness of her stomach. 'Not long now,' she assured him. 'Nina is due to go and get changed. When they've left, we'll slip off quietly. I do so want to be alone with you, Dominic,' she sighed out wistfully.

He pressed her closer to him until she could feel that hard imprint of his body against her back. 'Me too,' he murmured huskily. 'I've had enough of all this secrecy, darling. You looked so beautiful today, I wanted to shout out in church that you belong to me. I love you, Madeline.'

'Don't, Dominic,' she pleaded with him, glancing quickly around the room to see if they were being observed. But everyone's attention was on the bride and groom who were dancing their final dance before leaving the celebrations.

'Do you remember that last time we were all together in this room?' Dominic murmured suddenly. 'You came in through those doors, Madeline, wearing that exquisite lime gown, with your hair billowing about your shoulders and your eyes huge and frightened in your too pale face—and my heart stopped dead as I looked at you—you looked so hauntingly, tragically beautiful!'

Louise and her father had decided to hold the wedding reception at the country club because it was far better equipped to deal with the hundreds of guests they'd invited. Madeline's gaze took the journey she remembered taking that fateful night four years ago, and she sighed quietly.

'You were very angry with me, as I recall it.' She smiled a little sadly at the memory and leaned closer into the comforting frame behind her.

'I was a lot of things that night, Madeline,' Dom stated a little grimly. 'I was angry, yes, but I was also seething with the jealousy that seeing you in that young swine's arms filled me with, frightened by what was happening to us both—and so damned enchanted by you that I couldn't even control myself enough to leave you alone.

Perhaps if I had, things wouldn't have got so out of
hand as they did. By the time I took you on to the dance-
floor, I felt so battered by my emotions that I just let
rip with them.'

'We made a terrible scene that night,' she recalled.

'We certainly did,' he agreed. 'I don't think I've ever
felt so ashamed of myself as I did afterwards,' he added
grimly. 'But there you were, a tragic vision at my feet
in billowing silk, your beautiful head bowed in abject
remorse and—dammit, Madeline, but I could have sworn
you were mocking me!'

A smile touched her beautiful mouth. 'I was,' she said,
as she went to pull away from him. 'Look, Nina is ready
to go and change. I'd better——'

'What do you mean, you were?' he demanded,
grabbing her wrist to stop her running away.

Madeline turned, her dark hair twisted elegantly on
the top of her head, the Edwardian style of her cream
silk gown giving her that air of majesty the people here
in Lambourn had been forced to acknowledge as part
of the new and dauntingly sophisticated Madeline over
the last six weeks.

But the smile she laid on Dominic was old Madeline
to the core. 'You didn't think I would let you get away
with all those insults you'd thrown at me without giving
you something back by return, did you? Trust your instincts where I'm concerned, my darling,' she wisely advised. 'They're invariably right.'

'You were mocking me!' he growled.

'Of course,' she drawled, blue eyes mocking him even
now. 'I'll see you later, hmm?'

'Then why did you run away afterwards?' He wasn't
about to let her go until she'd told him everything.

Madeline levelled thoughtful eyes on him for a
moment. He was angry with her, and she hadn't wanted

that, not tonight. Tonight was supposed to be special. Their night—their secret night. 'Because,' she said quietly, very quietly, 'I knew you would never forgive me for that last trick. It was just too public—even for a bad Madeline trick.' Her mouth twisted in a moment of self-contempt then straightened again. 'You told me to grow up, remember? So I went away to do just that, and grow up I did.'

'But I'd forgiven you by the next morning, dammit!' he rasped. 'It was myself I had difficulty forgiving, not you!'

Without either of them being aware of it, Dominic's voice had risen, and already several people were glancing curiously their way, seeing another Stanton-Gilburn scene was in the making.

Then Madeline heard someone groan out an, 'Oh, no,' and recognised Vicky's pained voice.

Her eyes lifted pleadingly to Dominic's. 'Dom...?' she sighed in tired warning.

His gaze flicked impatiently around the suddenly quietened room, seeing what Madeline could not see since she had her back to the groups of people all watching them, and he let out a short sigh as he brought his wry gaze back to hers. 'Tell me,' he murmured quite casually, 'are you the new Madeline tonight, or the old one—only sometimes I find it impossible to tell the difference.'

Madeline pretended to consider the question before answering. 'A bit of both, I think,' she decided. 'I have been for several days now.' Her blue eyes teased him gently. 'It's almost as if the one sort of blended in with the other, one dark and stormy afternoon about two weeks ago, and since then I have difficulty myself trying to separate them.'

He laughed, not loudly but in a soft, indulgent kind of way, 'Well, whoever you are, I think I should warn you that there is a small convention of Stantons and Gilburns making their hurried way over here.' Once again his eyes flicked to a point just beyond her right shoulder then came back to her. 'I'm afraid it's truth or consequence time, darling,' he warned her drily.

'Oh.' Her lovely face lost its teasing smile. 'I didn't want this, Dom.'

'Then come here to me, and let me deal with it.' The hand still clasping her wrist drew her back against him and twisted into a strong hand-clasp, and by the time their two families arrived in varying stages of concern and irritation Madeline was being held securely at Dominic's side, his arm bent possessively around her waist so that their clasped hands rested on the flat of her stomach.

Edward Gilburn glanced from one studiedly expressionless face to the other, then muttered angrily, 'What the hell do you two think you're doing?'

Madeline turned a brilliant smile on the apprehensive Nina. 'Hello, darling! Shouldn't you be thinking of getting changed quite soon?' Her smile shifted to Charles. 'You'll miss your flight if you don't hurry.' There was still a small chance she could divert this, she thought hopefully.

But Perry joined the group, his hazel eyes enjoying the fun. 'Problems, anyone?' he innocently enquired.

'Not if these two are kept at separate ends of the room, no,' muttered Vicky, glowering at them.

'You have to be kidding,' Perry laughed, glancing down at their clasped hands then up at Madeline with a faint enquiry. She glanced at Dominic, also in enquiry, and he smiled down at her in rueful defeat. She looked back at Perry, also in rueful defeat, and everyone else looked at them in growing bewilderment. 'You may as well get it over with, you know,' he advised softly.

'Get what over with?' snapped Vicky impatiently.

'But this is Nina's day,' Madeline reminded Perry.

'And Nina has had a wonderful day, haven't you, dear?' Perry enquired of that sweetly bewildered bride. She nodded mutely, afraid to say a single word and instead stepping back into the sure comfort of her bridegroom's arms. Perry's eyes mocked the whole group. 'Look at their clasped hands, for God's sake!' he sighed out impatiently, but while everyone dutifully stared at their hands where the rich glow of gold mingled with the brilliant glitter of diamonds and sapphires, Perry was laughing into Madeline's and Dominic's rueful faces.

'We have an announcement to make,' Dominic said, and with the minimum of effort gained the full attention of the whole room. Madeline moved even closer to him, cheeks warming with a new and alluring shyness, and Dominic lifted their clasped hands to his lips, drawing her gaze up with them so that his eyes as he kissed her fingers showed her the burning depth of his love.

'Madeline and I...' he began, only to pause a second time, his smile taking her breath away before he gave his attention to their captive audience. 'Madeline and I....' he began all over again, his deep voice ringing out clear and proud across the silent room. '...married each other quietly a week ago...'

The low black Ferrari pulled up at the front of the old Courtney place, and Dominic withdrew the keys from the ignition and turned in his seat to look at the woman beside him. She was yawning, her head resting tiredly against the leather seat, eyes closed.

'Home,' he said with unbidden satisfaction.

'Mmm.' Her lips stretched into a sleepy smile. 'At least we didn't have to sneak off in the end.'

The news of their marriage had been supposed to be delivered by Perry after the celebrations were over and Dominic and Madeline had managed to make their escape. Things hadn't turned out quite like that.

A hand came to touch her cheek, gently caressing the satin-smooth skin so that her smile deepened into pleasure. 'Perhaps it was better that it turned out the way it did,' he pondered reflectively, 'even if we did succeed in causing yet another scene!'

'I suppose they'll blame it all on me,' Madeline complained. 'When this time, Dom, it was all your fault!' At last she managed to open her eyes so that she could glare at him.

He just smiled lazily. 'Sorry, darling.' The caressing fingers moved to her lips. 'I promise to make it up to you later.'

'We couldn't even manage to keep this place a secret,' she sighed.

'The house, you mean?' Dominic glanced into the darkness where the black and white painted house stood sheened by a silver moon. It still looked a rickety old place, even after all the work already done to it.

It had been Madeline's father who'd made the connection, turning to Dom with eyes turned as wicked as his daughter's as he murmured sardonically, 'Well, you must love her, Dominic, if you were willing to buy the Courtney place for her. Madeline always did love that funny old house.' And while the two men smiled ruefully at each other everyone else was gasping in horror, murmuring, 'The Courtney place? They're going to live in the old Courtney place?' as if they couldn't believe anyone with any taste could want to live there.

'It was only a matter of time before they eventually found out,' he pointed out, then, 'Come on.' He tapped her on the cheek. 'Let's go in.'

They met at the side of the car, Dom's arm going to rest across her shoulders as they stood staring up at the house. 'I'm sorry we don't have a resident ghost. It really does seem to need one,' he opined.

'And still could have,' Madeline declared with her usual optimism. 'After all, what self-respecting ghost would want to live among the tip we've made of it?' She waved a deprecating hand meant to encompass the whole inside where the dust lay thick and heavy over virtually everything but their bedroom. 'They've probably taken a vacation until all the work is finished, but they'll be back.' She turned in her husband's arm to gaze up at him, her blue eyes shining with wicked humour. 'You mark my words, the moment the last workman leaves here, our ghosts will return—and they'll haunt you, Dominic Stanton, for seducing a poor innocent maiden like me!'

He laughed, pulled her fully into his arms and leaning back against the car so that he could study her mischievous face. 'You're the one who haunts me, Madeline,' he confessed ruefully, 'and have been haunting me since the day you cast one of your wicked spells on me in my own swimming-pool!'

'That long?' She blinked up at him, black lashes flickering over her bright, teasing eyes. 'My poor darling.' Reaching up on tiptoe, she placed a consoling kiss on his smiling lips. 'How ever did you survive it?'

'Oh, I didn't mind,' he drawled. 'I used to let her phantom make mad passionate love to me every night— I rather enjoyed it, as a matter of fact,' he added lightly. 'I think I may even miss her now I've got the real thing to make love to me.'

'You prefer fantasy to the real thing?' she cried.

'I suppose it all depends on how the real thing measures up to her phantom,' he drawled provokingly, moulding her soft body into the hardness of his own. 'I've barely had a chance to compare them as yet.'

'Your fault,' she instantly laid the blame. 'You wanted us to marry in the crazily unconventional way. In fact, you insisted on it.'

'I wanted you!' he corrected gruffly, and suddenly humour had left him and in its place was a man full of grim-faced passion. 'And this time I wasn't taking any chances. Time and people and our own stubborn natures were our worst enemies four years ago. This time I was determined to get you tied to me before anything or anyone could so much as whisper an opinion! But,' he added heavily, 'it was only as I watched Nina walk down the aisle in her lovely dress that I realised what I'd deprived you of. I had no right to rush you into that civil wedding; you deserved the same fuss and——'

Her fingers covering his mouth stopped him. 'We had a lovely ceremony,' she assured him softly, her eyes warm with her love for him. 'Just you and I making our vows to each other with no one to intrude on the beauty of it. I don't feel deprived of anything, Dom—except perhaps having you hold me in your arms for the seven lonely nights since we married.'

'Then we have a lot of making up to do,' he agreed as he bent and scooped her into his arms. 'So let's get to it!'

The big black door opened and closed behind them. No lights came on inside. They didn't need them; their love was all they needed to light their way.

Outside the moon shone down on the old Courtney place, bathing its black and white walls in a pale silver sheen—and suddenly it didn't look such a rickety old place any more, but more like the proud and elegant dwelling the artist had captured on canvas all those centuries ago.

And, as if it knew that with these two caring people it would one day look just as it had used to look, the house itself seemed to give a contented sigh and settle back into its foundations, happy in the knowledge that it was loved again at last.

Next Month's Romances

Each month you can choose from a wide variety of romance with Mills & Boon. Below are the new titles to look out for next month, why not ask either Mills & Boon Reader Service or your Newsagent to reserve you a copy of the titles you want to buy – just tick the titles you would like and either post to Reader Service or take it to any Newsagent and ask them to order your books.

Please save me the following titles:	Please tick	✓
PASSION'S MISTRESS	Helen Bianchin	
THE UPSTAIRS LOVER	Emma Darcy	
BODY AND SOUL	Charlotte Lamb	
WAITING FOR DEBORAH	Betty Neels	
WILDFIRE	Sandra Field	
IN NAME ONLY	Diana Hamilton	
AN IMPORTED WIFE	Rosalie Ash	
BLAMELESS DESIRE	Jenny Cartwright	
MASTER OF DESTINY	Sally Heywood	
DANCE TO THE DEVIL'S TUNE	Lucy Keane	
LIVING FOR LOVE	Barbara McMahon	
DARK AVENGER	Alex Ryder	
WHEN STRANGERS MEET	Shirley Kemp	
PAST IMPERFECT	Kristy McCallum	
JACINTH	Laurey Bright	
HEIR TO GLENGYLE	Miriam Macgregor	

If you would like to order these books in addition to your regular subscription from Mills & Boon Reader Service please send £1.90 per title to: Mills & Boon Reader Service, Freepost, P.O. Box 236, Croydon, Surrey, CR9 9EL, quote your Subscriber No:................................... (If applicable) and complete the name and address details below. Alternatively, these books are available from many local Newsagents including W H Smith, J Menzies, Martins and other paperback stockists from 13 May 1994.

Name:...

Address:..

....Post Code:........................

To Retailer: If you would like to stock M&B books please contact your regular book/magazine wholesaler for details.

You may be mailed with offers from other reputable companies as a result of this application.
If you would rather not take advantage of these opportunities please tick box ☐

MILLS & BOON

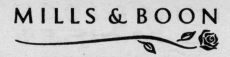

HEARTS OF FIRE by Miranda Lee

Welcome to our compelling family saga set in the glamorous world of opal dealing in Australia. Laden with dark secrets, forbidden desires and scandalous discoveries, **Hearts of Fire** unfolds over a series of 6 books, but each book also features a passionate romance with a happy ending and can be read independently.

Book 1: SEDUCTION & SACRIFICE
Published: April 1994   *FREE* with Book 2

WATCH OUT for special promotions!

Lenore had loved Zachary Marsden secretly for years. Loyal, handsome and protective, Zachary was the perfect husband. Only Zachary would never leave his wife…would he?

Book 2: DESIRE & DECEPTION
Published: April 1994   Price £2.50

Jade had a name for Kyle Armstrong: *Mr Cool*. He was the new marketing manager at Whitmore Opals—the job *she* coveted. However, the more she tried to hate this usurper, the more she found him attractive…

Book 3: PASSION & THE PAST
Published: May 1994   Price £2.50

Melanie was intensely attracted to Royce Grantham—which shocked her! She'd been so sure after the tragic end of her marriage that she would never feel for any man again. How strong was her resolve not to repeat past mistakes?

MILLS & BOON

HEARTS OF FIRE by Miranda Lee

Book 4: FANTASIES & THE FUTURE
Published: June 1994   Price £2.50

The man who came to mow the lawns was more stunning than any of Ava's fantasies, though she realised that Vincent Morelli thought she was just another rich, lonely housewife looking for excitement! But, Ava knew that her narrow, boring existence was gone forever...

Book 5: SCANDALS & SECRETS
Published: July 1994   Price £2.50

Celeste Campbell had lived on her hatred of Byron Whitmore for twenty years. Revenge was sweet...until news reached her that Byron was considering remarriage. Suddenly she found she could no longer deny all those long-buried feelings for him...

Book 6: MARRIAGE & MIRACLES
Published: August 1994   Price £2.50

Gemma's relationship with Nathan was in tatters, but her love for him remained intact—she was going to win him back! Gemma knew that Nathan's terrible past had turned his heart to stone, and she was asking for a miracle. But it was possible that one could happen, wasn't it?

Don't miss all six books!